Desperate

Caitlin stopped at the parking lot entrance, and cars worked around her. "I'm sorry, Nick."

"But you said you loved me. Is that something you turn on and off?"

"I just can't be with you."

"If you love me, I can change."

Caitlin said she wished she could believe that. Then she turned and started toward the oak tree where our group met every morning. She said she wouldn't tell anyone what happened.

Why was she doing this? I wanted to run, throw myself at her feet. Or maybe grab her shoulders and shake her until she begged me to stop. But she stood by Saint, their bodies perfect as puzzle pieces. I was the one who didn't fit. I trudged to my car. One thing was sure, I'd do anything to get her back.

ALSO BY ALEX FLINN

BREATHING
UNDERWATER

alex flinn

HARPER TEEN
lishers

The author spoke with several people and did extensive research regarding the various counseling and anger control programs available to batterers. The Family Violence Class in which Nick participates, while representative of the type of programs available in various jurisdictions, is fictional. It does not portray any particular program or group leader.

Breathing Underwater
Copyright © 2001 by Alexandra Flinn
www.epicreads.com

Library of Congress Cataloging-in-Publication Data
Flinn, Alex.
    Breathing underwater / Alex Flinn.
        p.   cm.
    Summary: Sent to counseling for hitting his girlfriend, Caitlin, and ordered to keep a journal, sixteen-year-old Nick recounts his relationship with Caitlin, examines his controlling behavior and anger, and describes living with his abusive father.
        ISBN 978-0-06-029198-3 — ISBN 978-0-06-029199-0 (lib. bdg.)
        ISBN 978-0-06-447257-9 (pbk.)
        [1. Dating violence—Fiction.   2. Anger—Fiction.   3. Fathers and sons—Fiction.   4. Child abuse—Fiction.   5. Diaries—Fiction.]   I. Title.
PZ7.F6395 2001   00-044933
[Fic]—dc21   CIP
                                                                                              AC

Typography by Adam B. Bohannon
12   13   14   15   CG/BV   10   9   8   7   6   5   4

Revised edition, 2011

ACKNOWLEDGMENTS

The author would like to thank the following people: Mariel Jones and Joan Farr, for sharing their experiences with Miami-Dade County's courts and counseling programs; Richard Peck, for getting me started; Felizon Vidad and Barbara Bottner, for helping edit my drafts; my husband, Gene, and my daughter, Katie, for their support; the members of my critique group, for all their encouragement; my mother, Manya Lowman, for always thinking I'd be a writer despite ample evidence (like my high school English grades) to the contrary; my editor Antonia Markiet, for her knowledge and experience and, especially, for listening; and my agent, George Nicholson—for being the best.

My special thanks to Joyce Sweeney, a great writer, teacher, and friend.

In memory of my father,
Nicholas Kissanis

JANUARY 5

Justice Building, Miami, Florida

I've never been in a courthouse before. But then, I've never been in such deep shit before, either. The metal detector screams when I walk through, and a security woman tries to check my pockets. I pull away.

"These what you want?" I dangle my keys an inch from her nose, getting in her face. She backs off, scowling. I throw them into her yellow plastic basket and walk through again.

"You were supposed to give me those first," she says.

"Sorry." I'm not.

Behind me, my father flings in his keys. "You're always sorry, Nicholas, always forgetting." Then, he looks at the security woman, and his expression becomes a smile. "Miss, if you would please be so kind to tell me where is this courtroom?" He hands her the notice for my hearing.

She smiles too, taken in like everyone else by his Armani suit and Greek accent. "Second floor." She looks at me. "Restraining order, huh?"

"Trouble with his girlfriend." My father shakes his head. "He is sixteen."

I stare forward, remembering a day on the beach,

Caitlin laughing, a white hibiscus in her hair. Was it only a month ago? God, how did we get here?

My father nudges me onto the escalator, and it bears me up, high above the white-tiled floors and the metal detector, far from the security woman's gaze. We reach the top, and he shoves me through a green door.

The courtroom smells like old books and sweat. Brown benches, like church pews, face the witness stand. On the front wall, gold letters read:

MIAMI-DADE COUNTY, FLORIDA
WE WHO LABOR HERE SEEK ONLY THE TRUTH.

Fine, if you know what the truth is. Caitlin sits with her mother in the center pew. Dressed in white, her blond hair loose, she looks like something from our mythology book, a nymph, maybe, pursued by a beast. Guess I'm the beast. I pass her.

"Why are you doing this, Cat?" I whisper. "I thought we had something special."

Caitlin examines her knees, but I can tell her eyes are brimming. "Yeah, Nick. I thought so too."

"Then, why—?"

"You know why." She moves to the other side of her mother.

I must stand there a second too long, because my

father shoves me forward. I take a seat in the fourth row. He leaves a gap between us, opens his briefcase, and removes a thick folder. Work. I try to catch his eye. "Do you think they'll—?"

His eyes narrow in annoyance. "Nicos, this is important." He gestures at the folder.

I look away. From across the room, I feel Caitlin's mom staring and Caitlin trying not to. So I concentrate, really concentrate, on making my face a mask. I'm good at that. People at school—my ex-friends, even Tom, who used to be my best friend—see me how I want them to: Nick Andreas, sixteen-year-old rich kid, honor student, coolest guy around. All fake. Only Caitlin knew the truth about the warfare with my father. She knew how humiliating it was warming the bench in football all season.

Telling her that stuff was a mistake. It's easier to fake it. When you fake it for sixteen years, it becomes part of you, something you don't think about. Maybe that's why I can hold a smile when the judge—a female judge who's sure to take Caitlin's side—enters and Caitlin takes the witness stand. I grin like an idiot as the bailiff swears Caitlin in and a lawyer in a gray polyester skirt begins asking her questions.

"State your name," the polyester lawyer says.

"Caitlin Alyssa McCourt."

Polyester points to the paper she's holding. "Is this your statement, Miss McCourt?" Caitlin nods. "You'll have to voice your answers for the record."

"Yes."

"Is it your testimony you were involved in a relationship with the respondent, Nicholas Andreas?" Yes. "Is he here today?" Yes. "Point him out, please."

Caitlin's finger stretches toward me. I meet her eyes, try to make her remember all the good times. Bad move. Her tears, brimming before, spill out, unchecked. A tissue is offered. Polyester keeps going.

"Was the relationship a sexual one?"

Caitlin's hands twist in her lap. "Yes."

"Was the sex consensual?"

Cat says nothing, glancing at her mother. The question takes me by surprise. Does she mean to lie about that too, make it rape, what we did together? It wasn't. Polyester repeats the question, and Caitlin says, "I heard you. I was thinking." She looks at her mother again and wipes another tear. Her chin juts forward. Finally, she says, "Yes. It was consensual. Nick and I . . . I loved him."

In her seat two rows away, Mrs. McCourt shakes her head. Now, Caitlin stares forward.

"What happened December 12?" Polyester asks.

I look at the wall, my attention suddenly riveted

by a palmetto bug, feelers writhing. I could kill it if I wanted.

"He hit me."

The bug slides to the floor.

I don't listen much after that, just watch Caitlin's mouth move. My father plunks a hand on my shoulder, saying something I don't hear. Anyone looking would think he's patting my back, but his fingers claw my skin. Excuse me, Your Honor, but I'm bleeding. *'Scuse me while I kiss the sky.* The lyrics run through my head with all the other suddenly meaningless information. Will this be over if I say it's all true? Deny it? Apologize? Cat's mouth moves until I wonder if she's reciting the alphabet, the Lord's Prayer, the Pledge of Allegiance. No way could she say that much bad stuff about me. But when I tune in a few seconds, I hear her, agreeing with everything Polyester says I did, not explaining, not giving any background, just agreeing. It was a slap, I want to tell them. One slap, when she pushed me way too far. I never beat her up, would never hurt her. I loved her, love her still. Doesn't she remember anything good about us? I do.

Caitlin clutches the tissue like a white flag. She doesn't use it again until Polyester's final question.

"Are you in immediate fear for your safety as a result of your boyfriend's actions?"

Caitlin wipes her eyes, but when she speaks, her voice is strong.

"Yes. I am."

Polyester has no further questions.

"You may step down," the judge tells Caitlin. Then, Madame Judge turns to me. "Anything you'd like to tell the court, Mr. Andreas? You aren't required to testify."

I'm on the witness stand before I realize what my father said before. "Don't say anything." I try to avoid his gaze, but I'm drawn to it by sheer will. He telegraphs a message: You're in big trouble, kid.

My father and I look alike. I don't remember my mother much—she left when I was five—but I'm sure I don't look like her. My dark hair and dimples come from my father's gene pool sure as the baby lizards running across our garden path look like Papa Lizard humping on the hibiscus. Still, I search the mirror for differences, anything to avoid seeing him in myself. His eyes are bad enough. Those green eyes can do more damage than his fist, and I see them in my own eyes every day.

Yet, it's my father's eyes I notice now, my father I'm trying to please when I speak on the witness stand, lying despite the oath. I wonder if God is listening, if God exists.

"I never hit her. Caitlin's making this up to get back at me for breaking up with her. She's nuts." My face hardens. The mask takes over. "She doesn't need a restraining order. She's flattering herself if she thinks I'd waste my time."

I start to step down, knowing I screwed up big-time. The judge's voice stops me.

"Stay there, Nick."

I sit. Where does she get off calling me *Nick*? A brass nameplate identifies her as THE HONORABLE DEBORAH LEHMAN. What if I called her Debbie, maybe even Debs? *So, Debs, what's your take on separation of powers?* It wouldn't matter. Judge Lehman is destined to hate me. Young, but not pretty, brown eyes swimming behind thick glasses. I see her as a schoolgirl, lenses covered in fingerprints, waiting for the day she can screw someone like me. Her next words prove my point.

"You think you're pretty cool, don't you?"

What can you say to that?

"You can stop with the *who me* look. You may think I don't know you, but I do. I see you every day, you and other boys like you in your Abercrombie & Fitch khakis, privileged boys who live on Key Biscayne and have everything handed to them."

Sounds like you're seeing things. But I don't let myself say it. Control is part of faking it.

"You're not the least bit sorry, are you?" Judge Lehman persists. "You tell me your girlfriend's crazy.

She's lying. Sweet little you could never do such a thing. Right, Nick?"

The mask doesn't like the direction this is taking. "Right."

"Wrong," Judge Lehman says. "Because you see, Nick, I can read minds. I see inside you, and I don't like what I see."

I fake a smile. "I'll get going then."

"Sit!"

Judge Lehman reaches for a paper on her desk. "I'll grant the request for a restraining order. If you contact Caitlin McCourt, talk to her at school, if you so much as look at her funny in the hallway, you go to jail. We understand each other?"

The mask constricts. Jail? For what? But I say, "That shouldn't be a problem."

Judge Lehman smiles a bit. "Good. To make sure it's not, I'm also ordering six months' counseling, classes on family violence and dealing with anger."

Six months for a slap. Well, that's fair. "Whatever."

"And since you're having a hard time understanding how you got into this mess, I want you to tell me. Along with your counseling, you'll keep a journal, five hundred words per week. In it, you'll explain what happened between you and Caitlin McCourt, from the first time you saw her until today. You can write your version or the truth. I don't care. I like fairy tales. I won't even read it unless you want me to. But every week, you'll bring that journal to class and show your counselor you've written, that you're thinking about what you've done. If you're very lucky, maybe you'll learn something."

"You can't just convict me based on my clothes," I say. "Ever hear of due process of law?"

"Smart kid." She looks surprised. "Did you give your girlfriend due process before you hit her?" Before I can answer, she bangs her gavel. "Court's adjourned."

I jump down from the witness stand and ram my fist into a wall. It doesn't go through, and it doesn't even hurt, but the bailiff threatens to call security. "Don't bother, I'm leaving." I storm up the aisle. Mrs. McCourt smiles. Cat watches my father, and when I glance over, I see why. His face looks like it's on fire. Still, I follow him out, my hand finally uncurled enough to ache.

We walk to the parking lot. The January air is barely cold, and my father's green Jag's parked between two spaces. He unlocks it, and I get in. He slams his door and shoves the key into the ignition.

"You had to talk, did you?" he says over the motor. "You just had to open your big, fat mouth."

His hand moves from the steering wheel, and I feel myself flinch. *Coward.* When I look again, his manicured fingers rest, harmless, on the gearshift. I say, "I'm sorry, Dad."

"You always are," he replies. "And yet, you always say the wrong thing, always the stupid thing. This is why you always fail."

I don't fail, I want to say. But, for an instant, I remember Caitlin's face, and I know my father's right about me.

"I didn't know what to say," I try to explain.

He flips on the classical station. Screeching violins fill the air, and the conversation's finished.

Later that day

To: Judge Debbie Lehman
From: One Rich Key Biscayne Kid in Abercrombie & Fitch
Re: My side of the story (as if you care)

That's what I've written so far, and I've been sitting two hours. I can't believe I have to write five hundred words a week. Five hundred words—that's like major literature. Having screwed around the last hour trying to decide whether to write in the style of Isaac Asimov (that version featured Caitlin as a Venusian chick with one eye and three breasts) or Dr. Seuss ("I am Nick/

Nick is sick/Nick tells Debbie to . . ." well, you get the idea), I need to get down to it. Though it means remembering things I'd rather forget, I finally decide to write the truth. It doesn't matter anyway.

Tuesday morning, second week of sophomore year, I approached Key Biscayne High's Mercedes dealership of a parking lot driving a red 1969 Mustang convertible, my father's belated birthday gift. Tom rode shotgun. His long blond hair blew in the breeze, and he pretended not to flex his muscles to impress whatever girls might notice. In other words, nothing unusual was happening, nothing to hint at what was coming: the end of Nick Andreas as I'd known him.

Tom and I had been best friends since first grade. That's when I'd figured out that Tom's peaceful house was the best place to escape my father. I didn't tell Tom that, of course. He'd never understand. It wasn't that I blamed Tom for getting everything he wanted. I couldn't do that because he was such a great guy. But then, we'd all be great guys if we had his life.

That day, he was trying to talk me into

asking out Ashley Pettigrew. I told him she wasn't my type.

This confused Tom. "Who cares?" he said. "She's hot for you."

I asked him if that was all he thought about.

Tom nodded and said, "That's what I like about you, Nick—no competition for girls. You're the only guy I know who actually aspires to die a virgin."

His words were still hanging like a cartoon bubble when I saw Caitlin. She emerged from the mob of JanSport-toting zombies. I stared a second. Then, a second longer. I knew her. The words dream girl, stupid and corny as they were, popped into my head. This was her. The One. It was ninety-three degrees out, but she didn't wear shorts like everyone else. She actually wore a dress. Still, I noticed the outline of her breasts, her legs brushing together. Other girls wore silver earrings shaped like crosses or hoops. Hers were pearls. She moved out of range, and I turned to Tom.

"That's the one I want," I said.

Tom was back to looking at his biceps. "Who?"

I pulled down Tom's arm and pointed. "The blond in the blue."

He looked. "Her? You're so kidding me. That's Caitlin McCourt. Remember, from kindergarten? And every grade after that."

"She didn't look like that in kindergarten."

"She went to fat camp this summer. Everyone's talking about it." He stopped staring at himself long enough to give me a funny look. "She's a geek, Nick. She's in chorus, for God's sake. And she'll get fat again."

I didn't answer. I was picturing the way Caitlin McCourt moved, walking away. I wanted to touch, even smell her. How would her skin feel under my lips?

Tom went back to talking about Ashley, and I'd get nowhere with him. So I eased into a parking space. I figured if I ran, I could maybe track Caitlin down before class. Not that I knew what I'd say. Leaving the top down, I sprinted to the building while Tommy Boy was still examining his pecs.

I put down my pen. Four hundred ninety-nine words is all I can manage. I'll write the extra word next week.

JANUARY 10

In my worst nightmares

I do not belong here.

Picture this: seven guys in a circle, like a prayer group or something, in a room that overlooks the Metrorail train tracks. The walls are covered with nightmares— wild modern art that looks like those old John Carpenter horror movies on late-night TV. The population is scarier. There's everything from a guy with pierced cheeks to a scrawny accountant type who looks like he made a wrong turn on the way to a Rotary Club meeting. We do have two things in common: First, we're all pissed about being in Family Violence Class. Second (I think I can go out on a limb), we're eyeing this guy across from me, who's staring at the floor and ceiling, eating his fingernails to the nub, and rocking back and forth. I try not to gawk. You never know what sort of weapons a psycho like that could have. But it's like a car wreck or a girl with enormous breasts. You have to look. Now he's clenching his fists, shaking.

I scan the room, mentally awarding the prize for Most Likely to Kill Someone in a Traffic Altercation. Six-way tie. Our instructor, a fat, cherubic-looking guy named Mario Ortega, explains the rules.

"I don't make many rules," he says. "Those I do

make, I expect followed. Arguments to the contrary, you can take to the judge."

He smiles quickly, like he's joking, but his eyes don't smile with him.

"Rule one," he continues, "is, be honest. Without that, there's nothing I can do."

"Honest," says a voice. "I don't do rules much."

This comes from the skinny blond kid two seats down. You know the type. Only an illegible tattoo keeps him from looking nine years old. He runs a pen-knife under filthy nails. It sounds clichéd to call him a redneck, except the back of his neck is at least bright pink. His face matches it. I'd bet there's a pickup truck with a gun rack out in the parking lot.

"You don't, do you?" Mario asks. "Well, if you have a problem, you can leave." Mario slaps a palm to his forehead. "Oh, I forgot! You can't leave. I guess we'll have to open our minds, Mr. . . ." Mario checks his list. "Mr. Kelly, I believe."

"Kelly's my first name," the redneck says, and I suspect from Mario's smile he knew that. Kelly glares at all of us, and I silently thank whatever deity was on duty the night my parents saw fit *not* to give me a girl's name. "No cracks if you know what's good for you."

"We don't put each other down here," Mario says, turning his attention back to the group. "That's another rule. The rest are pretty simple, and since you've got no choice, you'll follow them. Next one is, be on time."

As if on cue, the door flies open. The guy who opens it looks in no particular hurry. Like most of the group, he's about my age, but he's normal compared to the rest of them. Better than normal, maybe. Tall and dark, with a take-no-shit walk, he apologizes, his cool voice conveying no actual contrition, and sits by Kelly.

"How perfect," Mario says. "I was just explaining my quirk about punctuality." Mario consults his list again. "You must be our lost lamb, Mr. Sotolongo."

"Leo Sotolongo." Leo displays two rows of white teeth. "I'll be good from now on, Teach. Promise."

"Fine." Mario looks away before Leo finishes speaking. "Rule four: no drugs or alcohol. Rule five: participate in class discussions."

The Psycho across the circle stabs a pencil into his palm. It must hurt, but he doesn't even flinch. Me, I have no intention of talking. I have enough problems without some Ph.D. deciding the reason Caitlin and I fought has something to do with my father using me for a punching bag all these years. That's an old story. Been there, done that, heard it on *Oprah*. I figure the time spent here will be an excellent period to devote to Serious Thought—say, memorizing the periodic table of elements. The mountain of a black guy beside me—obviously a result-oriented individual—nails my feelings when he says, "We get a grade on this?"

The rest of the group nods as one, except the Psycho, who's still trying to impale himself on his number two lead, and Mario says, "Well, I guess it's pass/fail. You don't participate, I cut you loose. For you court-ordered people, that means starting over again. Or face the consequences."

The consequences being hard time. The big house, the pokey. Got the message. I nudge the big guy. "Notice he didn't say *how much* we had to participate?" He nods.

"That brings us to the most important rule." Mario eyes each face. I turn away, sure for a second he sees everything I don't want him to. "You will take responsibility for your actions. I'm not the court system or your girlfriends. So, I won't accept 'I was drunk' as an excuse. If everyone who got drunk beat up on someone else, we'd all have black eyes every day. And being plain old pissed off's no defense either. If you think your girlfriend's the biggest slut in the world, leave her. Don't hit her. *You* are responsible for your violence. You won't get better 'til you come to terms with that."

"But what if it really wasn't our fault?" The big guy echoes my thoughts again.

"How so, Mr. Johnston?"

"It's Tyrone. My friends call me Tiny."

Tiny weighs at least two fifty. His hair is shaved on the sides, and the sleeves of his Tasmanian Devil T-shirt are rolled back to expose his muscles. There are enough chains around his thick neck to drown someone smaller. What kind of damage could a guy that size do to a girl?

"I mean, I'm the one who's abused in my relationship," Tiny continues, cracking his quarter-sized knuckles. "Donyelle might look small, but she's got the power. Women always do. I told her if she kept beating on me, I'd do her some damage. Finally, I had to bust her mouth just to show I meant business." He flops his palms onto his lap. "They arrested the wrong person, but they don't care, long as they keep us people in line. And they pressed charges even though Donyelle told them we're engaged."

I feel myself nod. "I hear you," I say. Caitlin never hit me, of course, but what about mental torture? What about getting a guy so crazy he has to use his fists—hands—in self-defense?

"How'd you feel, hitting her?" Mario's voice comes through the crap in my brain.

"I didn't wanna hurt her," Tiny says. "But sometimes a man's gotta stand up for himself, right?"

"You said we were supposed to be honest!" a voice cuts in before Mario can answer.

The statement comes from the Psycho. While Tiny was talking, the Psycho's been doing some serious shaking. Now he looks up at us.

"What?" Tiny says.

"He said we're supposed to be honest."

"I am being honest!" Tiny straightens himself to his full height.

"No." The Psycho shakes his head a few times too many, but he's too crazy to be afraid of Tiny. "Not you, big guy. Me. 'Cause I don't know what honest is. I don't want to tell a lie, but I don't know." He takes head in hands, singing, "I don't know, don't know . . . don't know . . ." A tear oozes from each eye, and the guy to his right is on the corner of his seat. Mario comes between them, putting an arm around the Psycho's shaking shoulder.

"What's your name, son?"

"A.J.," he manages before beginning to sob again on Mario's shoulder, great heaving shudders. Mario whispers in his ear.

I tune them out. Hearing them might make me be like them.

Several minutes later, A.J. winds down, and Mario turns to us. "Anyone else feel like that?"

"Like what?" Kelly again. "I have no idea what this waste case is saying."

Mario shrugs. "Like your life's a big act. Like you're trying to be a man when you're just a scared kid, trying to keep under control when you really want to scream, cry, maybe hit someone. Ever feel like you're breathing underwater, and you have to stop because you're gulping in too much fluid?" A.J. begins to sob again. Mario gestures toward him. "This is what we were going to do anyway."

"What?" Kelly demands, folding the penknife. "Cry?"

"Reflect on the errors of our ways that landed us here, Kelly."

"Ain't it obvious? We all hit our girlfriends. Class dismissed."

"Not me," Leo, the guy who was late, says. "I didn't hit anyone."

"That's a laugh," Kelly says, snorting. "Spics all hit your women. Spic women think it's their mission to get hit."

"You mind repeating that?" Leo's fists clench.

Kelly sits upright. "You telling me your daddy don't hit your mama?"

Before Leo can answer, Mario says, "Enough! I know you're all tense, but that will be the last time we mention anyone's mother. Let's cool it with the ethnic slurs too."

"And if I don't?" Kelly says.

"You'll be spitting out some teeth, Miss Kelly." Leo answers for Mario. "Not that it won't be an improvement."

And Kelly's on top of him. Leo's up an instant later, one hand on Kelly's neck, holding him away from his body. He shoves Kelly into the wall. Chairs fly as we clear the way. Someone starts chanting, *"Fight! Fight!"* Others take it up. Kelly's gasping for breath. A vein bulges in Leo's forehead, but otherwise he holds Kelly like he's nothing. Mario steps between them, putting a hand on each of their shoulders and shouting, "Calm down," his voice becoming softer as he eases them apart.

"I'll have no violence in my group, Mr. Sotolongo," Mario says when Leo finally sits.

"You're blaming me?" Leo's voice is cold. "Little turd attacked me."

"I know that. I also know your record and the charges against you."

"Man!"

"I'll have no violence in my group," Mario repeats as the accountant bolts for the door.

And then there were seven.

It takes several minutes for everyone to calm down, but, finally, Leo's in a chair by mine, and Mario's next to Kelly.

"Go on, Mr. Sotolongo," Mario says. "You have the floor."

"That's it. I didn't hit anyone."

"What brings you here then?"

"You know the charges," Leo throws back at him.

"I'd like to hear your version."

"My version? My girlfriend's parents hate me."

"Why do you suppose that is?"

"'Cause I took it from her."

"It?"

"Her virginity," he says. "Mama and Papa wanted their baby to stay pure 'til she died, at least. Trouble is, she didn't want to stay pure." Laughs and nods from some of the group. "I screwed up their plans. I must've threatened her. Raped her." He tips back his chair. "Bullshit. She sold me out, lied so she wouldn't get in trouble. But I'll get Neysa to drop the charges." He smiles and flips his jacket collar. "So, I won't be coming here much longer."

Leo scans the circle, his eyes finally meeting mine, and suddenly I wish I was him, so calm, so confident everything will work out. At least, I want to be someplace else, not laying my life open to these assorted losers. But that isn't happening, so I stand.

"I never hit anyone either," I say, trying to replicate Leo's cool. "My relationship with Caitlin wasn't violent. It was damn near perfect."

"And you're here because . . . ?" Mario says. When I shrug, he says, "What does the court say you did? Start with your name."

I run a hand through my hair. "I'm Nick, sixteen, and like I said, I don't know why I'm here. I lost it once and slapped my girlfriend. That's it. One lousy slap."

I'm finished, and I start to sit. Mario stops me.

"What's a slap, Nick?"

"You don't know what a slap is?"

"I'm wondering how hard you hit her."

I shrug, but Mario's expression makes me answer seriously.

"Not very. A slap, like I said. Open hand. Her face didn't turn red or anything."

"So you hit her in the face."

"No. I *slapped* her in the face. Look—" I pace a few steps before I catch myself. "I shouldn't have, okay? I know that. But she pissed me off this one time. Once."

"What was the fight about?"

"It was stupid."

"So stupid you hit her? Doesn't sound stupid to me."

"It doesn't matter anymore. She hates me. None of my friends are talking to me, including a guy I've known since kindergarten, because of one crummy slap." I sit. Mario still dogs me.

"Sounds like your life is ruined, Nick."

"Pretty much."

"Don't you want to make sure it doesn't happen again?"

Mario leans across the circle, but I avoid his eyes. I hear blood pounding through my ears and I do feel like I'm breathing underwater. I touch the amethyst ring in my pocket, the one I bought Caitlin. "Whatever."

The Psycho—A.J.—bursts into tears again. I try not to look because looking makes me hear my father's voice—the voice that's always, always telling me how bad I screwed up, what a loser I am. I can't deal with his voice. And when I look past the pain in my head, there's Caitlin after it happened. The trust and everything she said she felt for me, gone. Over. "Whatever," I repeat.

I have to have Caitlin back. She's the only one who can silence the voice in my head.

Later that day

It's easier to pick up the pen this time. After all, Caitlin's all I think about anyway.

I didn't see Caitlin again until seventh period, which was fate. When I walked into Spanish class, Caitlin stood by Señor Faure's desk, holding a transfer. She chose a chair two rows ahead and one seat to the left of mine, the perfect angle for me to see her rest her hand against her cheek, or watch as the tip of her pen entered her mouth. God, I wished I was that pen. I wished, also, to be one-tenth as cool as people thought I was—cool enough to talk to her.

A few minutes into reviewing irregular verbs (which I already knew, thanks to our parade of Spanish-speaking housekeepers), I felt a nudge. Tom pushed his notebook toward me. He'd written:

Stop staring. You look like a serial killer.
Bite me, I wrote back.

His notebook was under my nose again:

OK. I wouldn't kick her out of bed. Are you going to ask her out?

I looked away. I'd been considering the question, but there were others. What would I say? What if she wasn't interested? Or had a boyfriend? What if I puked my guts up, and she couldn't hear me through the gurgling? What if she laughed?

After class, I shoved my book into my backpack and bolted. Tom followed, trying to convince me to talk to her. I told him I'd decided he was right. I'd pass on Caitlin. But Tom said like hell I would, after slobbering the whole hour. He blocked the door, saying, "Go for it, Nick. You're not that ugly, man."

I said he was pretty funny, for a corpse.

Tom said he'd take her, if I wouldn't. He ran a quick hand down the length of his hair and walked to Caitlin's desk. I ducked into the hall to watch the sea of humanity roll by. There were no windows there, so although it was bright outside, my mind was gray. I couldn't believe Tom would hit on a girl I liked. He'd get her too. Like I said, Tom got everything he wanted.

When we were kids, Tom and I used to

tell people we were twins. I wished it was true. My father would go on the warpath, and I'd head for Tom's. Did his family wonder why I came over so often? I tried not to care.

When we got older, I realized no one could ever mistake us for brothers. Sure, we'd started out the same size, but Tom kept growing. Now, girls regularly embarrassed themselves over him—hanging at his locker or giggling when he passed them in the hall. I figured he kept me around to pour Gatorade at his victory parties. Mostly, though, Tom's face filled two dozen picture frames at the Carters' house. Mine wasn't on anyone's desk.

And perfect Tom was talking to Caitlin. He didn't even like her, but she was sure to like him. I wouldn't stand a chance. I pushed the door open. She was laughing—big trouble for me.

Tom stood. "Caitlin, meet Nick. He wants to have your baby."

"Or we could just go to the mall," I joked. I started to walk away, but Caitlin caught my eye and held it.

27

"We can talk about it," she said, then seemed surprised at her one-liner. There was a long silence before words sort of tumbled out. "I saw you in the parking lot today. Cool car. Did you and your dad fix it up or something?"

"Something," I said, wondering if she'd noticed me or my car. I decided it didn't matter.

Tom suggested we discuss it on the way home.

"Does Nick want to give me a ride home?" Caitlin asked. She said it to Tom but kept looking at me.

Her eyes were blue. The room had cleared, and even the hallway was quiet. It dawned on me Tom hadn't asked her out, he'd been holding my place while I found my nerve. Caitlin was into me, not him. The planets were orbiting in a different order. I stopped myself from grinning. Cool Nick took over. I said, "Sure, if you want."

When we reached the car, Tom made a big deal of getting in back, legs bent up, so Caitlin could sit next to me. She chattered on about her defective tongue which, she swore, made it impossible to roll her r's. Her tongue looked perfect to me. Finally, Tom changed the subject. "Caitlin, you know Zack Schaeffer? He's giving a party Saturday, back-to-school. I'm taking Liana Castro. You two should go. We could double."

"You're taking Liana?" I said. She was one of the few girls not openly drooling over Tom.

"Now, who are you taking?" he asked, grinning.

Tom and Caitlin looked at me until I said, "You want to go?" hoping to sound like her answer didn't matter. "With me, I mean?"

"I knew what you meant. I'd like that."

And Caitlin smiled. I wanted to put her smile in my pocket to look at over and over.

JANUARY 17

My room

The second week of Mario's class, I oversleep, awakened only by thunder roaring across the beach. I'm late. I dress and run down the marble stairs, my hand brushing the butt of the ridiculous naked woman–shaped pillar on the landing. When I pull the front door open, rain slaps me in the face.

Where the hell is my car?

I gape a second, unmoving. Then, I run into the downpour, searching, like maybe the car's playing hide-and-seek with me. But it would be hard to miss a car that red. It's gone. I stand there, getting wet. Finally, I sprint back upstairs to my father's bedroom, planning to—I don't know—tell him? Impossible. That would mean waking him. Instead, I dial the police, still clutching my journal for class.

"My car's been stolen!" I start to describe it when I feel him standing over me. His familiar Greek accent is like nails on a blackboard.

"It was not stolen."

I hang up. "What? Where is it?"

I turn. My father's maybe an inch taller than me, which is short. Still, his voice fills the room, and he looks pretty happy for this early Saturday morning. That kind of happiness is a bad sign.

"I sold it," he says. "Someone at the yacht club offered a good price."

"But it was mine." Even as I say it, I know his answer. My throat tenses, but I'm not surprised. The hallway clock chimes eight-thirty.

"I paid for it." Like I knew he'd say. "It was my car."

It was a birthday present. But I don't say it. Instead, I say, "I have class in half an hour. For court."

"Have the housekeeper drive you to the Metrorail station."

I leave my keys on the hallway table.

The train station is five minutes away, on the mainland. But half an hour later, I'm still waiting on its raised platform. The place is deserted, and the rain shows no signs of stopping. Gusts of water soak my face, rattle the tracks. I lean forward to search for the train's white light against gray sky. Not there. I'll probably have to take the class over, and it's my father's fault. The hollow in my stomach grows, and somehow, even my hunger becomes his fault. If he'd sold the car because of what happened with Caitlin, I'd understand. He didn't, though. He sold it because he could. The train finally lumbers in, and I get on.

The sagging seat hits my butt, and I stare through a dirty window.

I don't know when I first knew my family was different, that I could never tell anyone about the silences and the rages in my father's *Architectural Digest* house. I knew for sure when I was eleven, the year my father bought the Mustang. I came home one day to find my father smiling. Smiling. He was like a kid with a new toy, and for once, for once, he wanted me to play with him. I followed him to the garage, and there, beside his gleaming Mercedes, was a rusted-out carcass of a car.

"We will fix it together?" he said.

I nodded, though part of me—the smart part— knew it wouldn't happen. Like I said, I was eleven. I knew stuff. It was a good day. There were some good days then. But the smart part of me knew. Working on that car was something other fathers and sons did, something Tom and his dad did, not us. Not me.

I was right. A week later, he hired some grease monkey to replace the engine and just about everything else until finally, the car was perfect. My father liked perfect. Then, he hardly drove it.

Father's Day, I got the brainy idea of detailing it for him. I hitched a ride to the mainland for supplies then begged off the beach with my friends and spent the hotter part of a Saturday spreading Turtle Wax, rubbing it down with an old, soft shirt that still smelled of my father's cologne. I remembered him smiling the day he got the car. When he came home, I showed him what I'd done.

In the garage's fluorescent light, my father inspected my handiwork. Planets hesitated. He ran an index finger across the hood, opened doors, examined Armor All—coated rubber. Then, he circled the car to the other side, his entire body registering begrudging approval. On the passenger side, he stopped. He leaned over, eyes riveted to the door panel.

"What is this?" His green eyes barely flickering between the door and my face.

"What?" I stooped, saw nothing.

He jabbed his finger closer to the nothing. "That!"

A scratch. To call it a nick would grossly exaggerate its size. More like a paper cut, and one that must have been there to begin with. I'd been too careful. But my father wasn't rounding up suspects, and my butt was there to kick.

He never drove the car again. It went into hiding, and so did I. From then on, I avoided him, made good grades, and kept my room clean enough to perform surgery. It worked except when it didn't.

The car reappeared this past birthday. Birthdays are

hit-and-miss with my father, but this year, he remembered only a week late. Possibly, he'd been waiting for the occasion to remind me of my screwup. I came to breakfast, and he tossed me the keys on his way upstairs. "You break it, you own it," was his birthday greeting. It took me ten minutes to find the scratch before I drove to school, his words ringing in my ears. *You break it, you own it.*

Apparently not.

The train pulls into the Coconut Grove station. It's raining too hard for an umbrella to help, and I'm walking too far. The wind pushes at me like a defensive lineman and, finally, I ditch the umbrella and run to class.

I get there at nine thirty-five. Leo's standing, yelling at Mario. "Who are you to psychoanalyze me? I won't even be here next week."

Seeing me, Mario holds up a chubby paw and starts the standard teacher line, "Nice of you to join us—"

"Skip it," I say. I can't deal with this. "Just tell me where to retake the class. Better yet, throw me in jail. Who cares?"

I'm dripping bathtubs on the floor, so I turn to leave. Mario stops me. "You don't have my permission to leave."

I stop, glare at him.

"You're disturbing the class." He tosses me a roll of paper towels. "You're required to be here, so dry the floor and yourself, and sit down. We'll discuss your future here later."

I tear off a wad of towels, throw them onto the linoleum, and move the sopping mess with my sneaker, feeling Leo's black eyes on me. I glare back. Who does he think he is? I'm not towel-drying myself in front of this group, and I'm not explaining why I'm late, so I take a seat, feeling the blast of air-conditioning on my wet T-shirt. I shiver, and there's Leo-the-cool smirking in his chair. Suddenly, I hate him, hate him because he's got a girlfriend who'll drop the charges. Mine won't speak to me on a bet. Hate him because if we'd met in school, maybe we'd have been friends.

"Want a sweatshirt?" Mario gestures toward a Miami Hurricanes shirt draped across his chair.

"I don't wear orange," I say, and Mario turns back to the group. I sit, shivering through the rest of his lecture.

After class, I wait by Mario's desk until everyone else leaves. Leo gives one final smirk. I manage a sneer back. I examine Mario's photographs. There's a smiling woman, a little boy. Mario's family. What could he possibly know about my life? I'm about to ask him, but he speaks first.

"You want to talk about it?"

"I won't be late again, okay?"

"Fair enough. I'm sure you had a good reason." He smiles, fat cheeks spreading, and gestures toward my dripping notebook. "Are you writing in that?"

"Huh?" How'd I get off the hook so quickly?

"Your journal?"

"Oh. Yeah. Need to see it?"

"Maybe next week, when it's dry." Mario gathers his things, an umbrella, the sweatshirt, then turns. "My uncle Gustavo, a very wise man, used to say it doesn't take a genius to come in from the rain." I must look at him funny, because he adds, "Need a ride home, son?"

I've been looking out the window. It's eleven o'clock, but outside is night, with rain pounding worse than before. Still, I say, "Someone's picking me up."

After he leaves, I walk to the train.

Much later that day, after I (and the journal) have dried off

I look at my journal, hoping Judge Lehman doesn't require neatness. It's trashed—wavy and bumpy and smudged, like it's been through a shipwreck. Yet, I've dried it off with a hair dryer so I can write in it. Thinking of the car makes me think about Tom.

The day of Zack's party, I spent most of the afternoon waxing my car. Tom even helped. Buffing worked his triceps or something, and we were getting tan, too. He'd given up on Ashley and me, possibly realizing, before I did, that I was in love with Caitlin. Sometimes, Tom knew me better than I knew myself.

And sometimes, he didn't.

"Man, you're so lucky to get this car," Tom said. He was always saying stuff like that, and I never corrected him. I just sprayed Armor All and shrugged. Tom went on about what a perfect make-out machine it was.

I hoped so. I'd sort of been obsessing about kissing Caitlin that night.

Don't get me wrong. I was hardly sweet sixteen and never been kissed. I'd probably swapped spit with a dozen girls if you counted Spin the Bottle and a botched attempt to cop a feel off of Peyton Berounsky playing Seven Minutes in Heaven in eighth grade. By ninth grade, everyone was pairing off, at least for the evening, and I'd spent many sticky nights playing tonsil hockey on someone's parents' unsupervised sofa. So I'd touched, kissed, and groped, and been touched, kissed, and groped, all meaningless so far. I had a feeling Caitlin's would be the kiss that mattered.

That night, we had dinner in the Carters' dining room. Tom's family always ate there on weekends. I'd been joining them since grade school. The first time, I'd stood, gaping at the china, silver, and flowers, and Tom and his brother, wet-combed and shining. It was the kind of spread my father had for clients, not for me. They even dressed for dinner, although Tom and I just wore khakis. Conversation was quiet, smooth as peanut butter.

Like every time, Tom's old cocker spaniel, Wimpy, played around my feet. Feeding him table scraps was firmly against the rules, but for some reason, it was important to me to be Wimpy's favorite. I used to pretend he was my dog too. I listened to Mrs. C. describe the antics of Little Win, Tom's brother's baby, as I slipped Wimpy a huge bite of steak.

I got nailed. "Nicky, that's why that dog begs," Mrs. Carter said. I knew she was thinking about Labor Day, when Wimpy had put his whole face in the potato salad.

"And that's why he always wants to sleep on your bed when you stay over," Tom added. That always bugged Tom.

I apologized, but when they glanced away, I accidentally dropped another piece.

Over dinner, Tom's dad tried to talk us into working after school at his office. Tom rolled his eyes. We went through this every month, Mr. Carter trying to encourage Tom's interest in the family firm, and Tom avoiding the subject. Finally, Tom's mother rescued him, saying she was sure Tom had the rest of his life to work at a law office.

"Perhaps over the summer," Tom's father said.

Tom pretended not to hear. "Did I mention the Iceman has a date?" he said between forkfuls of potatoes. Tom was on a carbohydrate kick that week, although the week before, it had been proteins.

Mrs. Carter turned to me, glad to change the subject. "Is it anyone special?"

"I don't know yet. It's our first date." I was lying.

Tom mentioned she'd had lunch with us three times during the week, and his mom chuckled. "And what about you, Thompson? Who's your date?"

"I don't have one," Tom answered, before I could say anything.

I caught the look on Tom's face. Though I didn't know why, I changed the subject. "Did Trey send over any more pictures of Little Win?" I could always charm his mom.

Of course there were more pictures, so I told her we'd clear the table while she went and got them. I rose and picked up my plate. Tom followed me into the kitchen. When we were out of earshot, I asked why he hadn't told his parents about Liana.

"They wouldn't like it. Mom would hear a Cuban name and freak." Tom picked a leftover roll from the basket and downed it in two bites. "My parents' ancestors came over on the Mayflower, as Mummy likes to mention. They wouldn't want me dating anyone whose people floated in on less exclusive boats."

Rafts, he meant. Like in the newspaper—balseros, who swam from Cuba with nothing but the clothes on their backs and rafts made of driftwood and garbage. But what did that have to do with tall, beautiful Liana and her Tommy Hilfiger wardrobe?

"They wouldn't think that," I said. "Your parents are cool, and Liana's no boat person. She doesn't even have an accent. She grew up here."

"She was born here. It won't matter. Either her family's in the country club, or they're not. And if they aren't, they're not good enough for a Carter." Tom grabbed a handful of rice cakes. "My brother went to law school and married some cold fish from the Social Register, even turned down New York law firms to work for my dad. Now, I'm supposed to do the same thing, cut my hair, and conform. Forget what I want."

He didn't just mean Liana. I was sure of that. Only I knew that Tom secretly dreamed of becoming an artist, something else he'd never shared with his parents. His father dreamed of a law firm called Carter, Carter, and Carter, and Tom never told him otherwise. I said, "You're not being fair," meaning the art, more than Liana. "You should give them a chance."

"You don't know what they're like. They're not your parents."

No. They weren't, unfortunately. I shrugged, guessing I didn't know much about family relations. Leaving Tom in the kitchen, I pushed through the dining-room door. The Carters waited, packages of baby pictures spread before them. Mrs. Carter waved me over, pointing at a photo.

"Isn't he an angel?" she said. "Look at this one, with the bunny ears."

I nodded, but I was back to imagining Caitlin's kiss.

Key Biscayne High

Between Mario's class and writing in my journal, I'm still going to school. Everything's the same as always here, just not for me. The school office rearranged Caitlin's schedule so she seems like a figment of my imagination: no classes together, barely passing in the hallway. God, I miss her. I try sometimes to see her, making it look accidental. Like today. I go down where my locker was B.C. (Before Caitlin), on the first floor by the Fruitopia machine. She's there with all my ex-friends, laughing with Tom and Saint O'Connor, her blond hair barely visible between their massive forms. Saint is Key's star quarterback and also Tom's new best friend. What could he have said to make Caitlin laugh?

When I walk by, she stops laughing. Her eyes meet mine, but she makes the type of sound you'd get seeing a palmetto bug or some other vermin.

Tom sees me too. His eyes are the same as always, and for a second, I think he'll smile, say hello. Like, maybe things will just get back to normal. No way. Tom slips a hand onto Caitlin's shoulder. "Don't worry, Cat. Saint and I—we won't let him hurt you." The three of them glide as one toward the science wing.

I walk the other way, through the throng of what

used to be my friends. They ignore me. After everything happened with Caitlin, me hitting her, the restraining order, everyone took Caitlin's side. It didn't surprise me, except for Tom. Tom, who knew me better than anyone, who should have stood by me. I glance at Tom's back as they walk away, his fingers still on Caitlin's shoulder. How could he just toss a ten-year friendship over this? He wouldn't even talk about it. I guess it's like they say: When the going gets tough . . . your best friend flakes on you. So, who needs him? I should be glad he's not around.

I walk into English class. Heads turn. It's a small group, all honor students, and usually they're too busy yakking about the next Brain Bowl or Debate Team bagel sale to notice much. Today, silence. Every eye turns, in synch, from my face to the blackboard. I look, too, then turn away. Someone's written:

GO NICK! BEAT YOUR GIRLFRIEND!

I walk, seconds multiplying like amoebas, to my desk. Elsa, Caitlin's best friend, glares at me from under her beret—she has the nerve to wear that and look down on *me*? The rest just stare. Amy Patterson, who's had a crush on me since fifth grade, pretends to be fascinated with her grammar book. Trust me, she's faking it. But that's the closest anyone comes to taking my side.

The desks in here are arranged in a U shape so Miss

Higgins won't have to navigate rows in her motorized wheelchair. My seat faces the board. I shove my backpack under the chair, grip my desk sides, and stare at the green board until the letters blur and it's all black. I hear a voice.

"I wrote it, Nick. Why don't you hit me?" It's Elsa. And another girl, a new girl whose name I don't know:

"I wrote it, Nick. Teach me a lesson."

Derek Wayne, from across the room:

"I wrote it. Or do you only hit women?"

I want to bolt. Last week, Mario said if you think you're about to lose it, take a walk. I can't. I hold my desk like a life raft. If I go ballistic, they'll think they're right. *Be cool.* Mario's deep-breathing exercises and his rules rise, unbidden, in my mind. *Cool.* I think of icebergs, of ski trips with Tom's family when I'd refused to wear long underwear. I think of Leo. I think of breathing underwater. Finally, through the blur of thoughts and anger, I see Miss Higgins wheel through the doorway. A second later, she notices the blackboard. She sees, but it's too high for her to erase. She faces us.

"Who wrote this?" She scrutinizes us, acknowledging me before moving on. I keep breathing. Higgins tries again.

"Will the creative writer please identify him- or herself."

No one. Her eyes scan the room and finally land on Elsa. "Please erase it, Elsa."

Elsa hesitates, starts to speak.

I say, "Leave it."

Miss Higgins's eyes meet mine with a look I can't figure out. "Very well. But whoever wrote it neglected the comma."

She reaches above her head and chalks one between *GO* and my name. Whether she's deflecting attention or digging me a deeper hole, I laugh with the others. It sounds real. Then, to complete the illusion, I smile, raise my hand like nothing's wrong. When Higgins calls on me, I point to my copy of *Wuthering Heights*.

"Miss Higgins, in chapter three, when Cathy's at the window, is that supposed to be a ghost, or is Lockwood still dreaming?"

Higgins raises a sparse eyebrow. "What do you think, Nicholas?"

I can't go on like this, that's what I think. Losing Caitlin was bad enough without everyone hating me. And suddenly, my thoughts return to Tom. Talk to Tom. Years of friendship must be worth something. If I could only get Tom to forgive me, everyone else would follow. And with Tom's help, maybe I could get Caitlin back too.

46

But I say, "I guess it was a ghost. Like, maybe if people are in love like Cathy and Heathcliff, nothing can separate them, not even death."

Beside me, Elsa snickers, but I ignore her. I finger the ring in my pocket and reach under my desk for the journal. I don't care about English. I just want to remember when things were better. Like that first night with Caitlin.

The driveway to Zack's house was two blocks long, and since we were late, we walked it. Five minutes of gravel crunching under sandals. Finally, the trees parted, and Caitlin gasped. I let myself grin. The invitation was a lot of what I had to offer Cat. I got invited to all the cool parties. I'd hoped she'd be impressed. The house was huge, white, like the Disney version of a Southern plantation.

Caitlin looked from the house to my face. "I didn't know Zack lived someplace like this. I've known him all my life, but I never thought he was . . . rich."

She said the word like it burned her throat. I snuck closer, still unready to make the grab for her hand. I told her

Zack's family had just hit it big the year before.

"That explains why Zack blows off his old friends," she said, then added, in response to Tom and Liana's questioning looks, "He started hanging out with you guys, and now, he won't talk to me or Elsa, people he's known since kindergarten."

I told her no one really liked Schaeffer. We only let him hang with us because he had a hot tub and minimal adult supervision.

Caitlin said, "I get it. But for once, I'd like to be the one blowing people off instead of the one being blown off."

"A noble goal," I said. I threw open the front door and led her into a white-and-glass living room big enough for a pep rally. We walked through French doors to the patio. The hot tub was full of people in bathing suits that might come off before the evening was over. Almost everyone else circled the inkblot-shaped pool, though a few lurked in a corner, smoking grass. I avoided that area—one thing I don't do is drugs. Tom patted my backpack.

"What's in here?"

I told him beer, wondering if Caitlin would disapprove. Maybe I hoped she would. I mean, I didn't want a girl who drank. Still, I added, "I just wrote cerveza on Rosa's shopping list, and here it is."

"You the man!" Tom laughed, then added, to Liana, "Rosa's the housekeeper. What is she, Nick, number twenty-five?"

"Thirty-two," I corrected.

"So hard to find good help," Liana said.

I ignored her, watching Peyton walk by in a bikini that barely covered her nipples. She had rings on her toes and in her belly button, and Saint O'Connor, Key's Neanderthal star quarterback, followed, dragging his tongue on the ground. How could he let Peyton wear that in public? Caitlin, I noticed, wore a long skirt with a white linen shirt knotted over her tank swimsuit. Good. Though I wouldn't have minded seeing her in an outfit like Peyton's, I didn't want anyone else to. I swung my arm, fingers touching hers. For an instant, I saw her shiver. I grabbed her hand. She laughed then smiled at me, and even in the darkness, I felt my skin broil.

"Want to go swimming?" I asked, figuring

a shock of cold water would do me good.

"If you do," she said.

"I don't care." I led her to a stone bench, still cradling her fingers like feathers. Why was I so jacked up just holding this girl's hand? I told myself to chill.

Caitlin's eyes scanned the patio. "Good. I hate bathing suits. At camp, I always thought people were staring. And the girls here are so beautiful."

I squeezed her fingers. It was so cool that she didn't know how pretty she was. When I found my nerve, I said, "You're the most beautiful girl here."

She rewarded me with a smile. We stared at each other, me palming a Bud Light can until I felt a big paw on my shoulder. I smelled Doritos, saw red hair, teeth coated with orange cheese crap. Saint O'Connor. I put the can down. Saint raised a big arm to high-five, then clasped my hand instead.

I knew he was just looking for beer. I pushed my lips into a smile and withdrew my hand from Saint's and the other, more reluctantly, from Caitlin's. I handed Saint a can, offering Caitlin another. She shook her head. Saint looked like he'd just noticed her.

"Caitlin McCourt!" He whistled, two fingers to his mouth. She turned away, giggling. "Man, you are one hot babe. You must've lost thirty pounds at least."

"Thank you, Patrick."

Patrick? _Patrick?_ I felt my jaw clench. I'd never suspected O'Connor had a real name. How did Caitlin know? I chugged my beer, wanting to tell him to leave Caitlin alone. She was mine. But O'Connor was a football player who could pick his teeth with my arms.

I asked him if Peyton wanted one. Saint said, "Nah, she don't drink nothing with calories. I'll take hers, though."

Like I was buying drinks for this Saint Bernard. Maybe he figured I'd just hand over Caitlin too. But I pulled a beer out, yelled "Catch!" and hurled it over O'Connor's head so it splashed into the pool. Saint stood, blinking. Then, he turned to watch it sink.

I said, "Nice catch. Makes me glad you're on my team."

"Yeah, great throw, Andreas."

I said I didn't claim to be a star quarterback, and Saint smirked, like it was a good thing I didn't. I pointed toward the drowning Bud. "Mind getting that?"

"Be a sin to waste it." Saint nodded at Caitlin, then dove for his prey.

I thumbed open another can, pool sounds buzzing my ears like a traffic jam. Finally, I said, "How'd you know O'Connor's name?"

Caitlin laughed. "Patrick? I've always called him that. We had Sunday school together before I quit to join the church choir."

I rolled the icy beer in my hand. "You like him?"

"What do you mean?"

"Figure it out."

Her eyes widened. "Me and Pat O'Connor? That's so not possible. I mean, he used to burp and blow it on me." Her blue eyes focused on my face. Below, Saint and Peyton played chicken with Tom and Liana, Peyton fighting dirty, trying to pull off Liana's bikini top, Liana's shrieks echoing off the patio roof. But I heard Caitlin. "Besides, I like you, Nick."

The noise stopped. The ice melted, and I regained my sense of taste. I looked at her and said the first thing that popped into my head.

"You're in church choir?"

She made a face. "I bet you think that's so geeky." I shook my head, no, it suited my image of her, and she added, "I want to be a professional singer someday."

"What, like a rock star?" Which didn't suit her at all.

"I don't know, maybe. I take voice lessons, and I tried out for show choir last year, but I didn't make it. My mom said, 'It's because you're fat. No one wants to look at a fat girl, Caitlin.'"

"Nice mom," I said, feeling, if possible, closer to her.

"I know, but she was right. I lost thirty-five pounds, and then you asked me out."

"Making it all worth it?"

I swear, I was joking when I said that, but she said, "Kind of," smiling but serious. "I _did_ have the biggest crush on you in seventh grade. You gave that report on alternative power sources in Mr. Ohlfest's class."

I said I couldn't believe she remembered that. I moved closer.

She said, "I thought you were so smart, so . . . you didn't notice me, of course."

"I didn't notice anything in seventh grade. I still thought I'd play pro football in seventh grade." I rolled my eyes. "That was nice, actually."

She laughed. "You wouldn't have noticed me anyway."

Her fingers touched mine, and I leaned toward her. "I notice you now." I reached to caress her cheek, my lips an inch from hers.

"¡Oye, Nick! Caitlin!" Liana's voice was like the splash of cold water that followed. Caitlin and I separated, looking at the pool where Liana and Tom were locked in chicken-fight combat with Peyton and Saint. They were losing ground quick. Liana shrieked at us to help them.

I didn't move. They splashed harder, screaming for us to join them. After a monsoon drenched her skirt, Caitlin said, "Guess we have to."

I tried to stop her, but she stripped

to her bathing suit and slid into the water before I could see much of her. I looked at the spot where she'd been sitting, then down at the pool, and it dawned on me that there I could touch her like I was dying to. God, her legs would be around my head. I tore off my shirt and leaped in.

We didn't last long in the fight. Caitlin slipped from my shoulders in seconds. "Sorry," she sputtered, hugging herself and jumping side to side.

"Don't be." I moved closer, feeling her leg against mine. Droplets of water ran down her chest and beaded on her breasts. I'd die to touch them. Would she let me? Not likely. Still, for one moment, everything was possible. I fingered her waist then wimped out. "So it's just you and your mom then?"

"Yeah. Like you and your dad. Ever wish you had brothers or sisters?"

"No. I've got Tom. <u>He's</u> my brother."

She nodded. "I'm the same with my friend, Elsa."

I waded closer, my hand more firmly on her waist. "Know what I was thinking before we went swimming?"

"I think so." She looked into the water. "I thought maybe you were going to kiss me."

"Really?" I raised her chin, whispering, "I thought so too."

Suddenly, there was a crash. It came from the house, like a bus hitting a brick wall. Caitlin and I separated. We cleared the pool and ran through the maze of rooms.

Mayhem. Total mayhem. We stood, dripping, in the Schaeffers' bright white dining room. Except it wasn't white. Someone had spray-painted all over it. Chairs were overturned, backs broken off. The crash had been the chandelier. It lay between the table legs, having broken through the glass top. Crystal shards carpeted the room. In the center were three guys from school, juniors. They wouldn't have been invited. All had greasy hair and tattoos. One wore a goatee, another a dog collar with I LOVE SATAN painted on. They were pretty cut up from the chandelier. Still, they giggled like maniacs.

"Come on in, water's fine," said the guy with the goatee. His name was Dirk. I recognized him from junior high, where he'd spent assemblies picking his zits and eating them.

"Oh God," Caitlin whispered next to me. I slipped my arm around her. Then, people went in all directions. Someone, Tom maybe, looked for Zack. Some pushed through and joined in the trashing. Within seconds, they'd laid waste to the living room too. Most of us just stood there. But Caitlin looked frightened, so I tried to guide her back toward the patio.

"No," Caitlin whispered. Then, louder, so everyone heard. "No, you can't do this. You can't just trash someone's house."

The chaos stopped. Everyone stared at Cat like she was from outer space. Dirk came at her, stoned and cursing. He eyed Cat in her still-dripping swimsuit.

"We're just having fun, baby." He touched her waist. She made a sound like a hurt bird. "We could have fun with you, you little—"

He didn't finish. He didn't finish, because my fist met his jaw. Then, I was on top of him, waling on him, not seeing his face, just the paint-mottled walls and Caitlin. And Dirk's hand, touching her, hurting her. My breath in my ears drowned out the crowd sounds around me. Glass splinters ripped my skin. My fists flew, hitting and hitting him until finally his face was the colors of those walls, and I felt arms lifting me off him. Tom. It was then I noticed Dirk had stopped fighting. He moaned, so he must have been conscious.

Tom told me to get up. Zack had called the police.

Cat stared. I looked down and saw what she was looking at. Blood. Splinters of glass jutted from my arms, and my body was speckled red. Funny thing, it didn't hurt. But had I screwed things up with Caitlin? She took my hand wordlessly. I followed her through the white-tiled halls to the bathroom and sat on the closed toilet seat. She ran her fingers down my arms, looking for glass. I flinched.

"Does it hurt a lot?" she asked.

"No. I'm sorry, Caitlin. I screwed up. I saw him touching you, and I lost control. I couldn't stand—"

She put her fingers to my lips. "Don't apologize. It's so incredible what you did. No

one's ever fought for me, but you . . ." Her
voice trailed off. She stroked my arm, picked
out each shard of glass in her way, then
used a washcloth to blot the blood. I relaxed
under her touch. For a second, I was four
years old, going to my mother with a skinned
knee and having her tell me not to be a baby.
But now, it was Caitlin's face, her voice in
my ear, whispering, "You're a hero, Nick.
You're my knight in shining armor."

I stood. My arms still bled, but I didn't
care. I pulled her close.

I was right. Hers was the kiss that
mattered.

That night, in bed

I flip through the journal again, remembering. Funny,
how I can remember stuff that happened months ago,
even little things she said or did, like it was yesterday. I
guess it's 'cause she's still so important to me.

I put down the journal and reach for my clock radio.
The same words were written on the blackboard fifth
period and again in seventh. There, the teachers erased
it, but since Higgins doesn't use the board, it stayed
there all day. I set the alarm to go off an hour early. I'll
get to school by seven to obliterate the words.

JANUARY 26

Spanish class

Tom stares at me.

I'm in Spanish class Monday, flipping through the pictures I took of our group in Key West. Nothing interesting on the blackboards lately. Still, I need to talk to Tom. Across the room, he laughs with Saint O'Connor, sitting in what used to be my seat. I look back at the photographs.

The Key West trip was two months ago, Thanksgiving weekend. But in my mind, it plays like video of someone else's childhood. There's Caitlin and me silhouetted against the sunset at Mallory Square. Another is the group in front of Zack's parents' vacation house. I took that one, so I'm not in it. But there's one of Tom, Saint, and me pretending to dive at the sign that says SOUTHERNMOST POINT IN THE CONTINENTAL UNITED STATES. The images surprise me now. Was I that person? An hour at the Walgreen's lab made it so.

I look longest at a picture Caitlin took, Tom and me on Zack's boat. We're waving our diving masks, best friends. I take that one out, along with three group shots. The one of Tom and me goes on top.

"Señor Andreas, you are doing your workbook, no?" Señor Faure has noticed my inattention.

"I'm finished," I say.

"Work ahead, then. Do the next chapter."

"I finished the book. Want to see?"

A few giggles at my nerdliness. Faure shrugs. "Do something quiet, then."

"That's what I was doing."

Faure nods, and I smile at Jessica Schweitzer, who sits next to me. She looks away. I pull a sheet of paper from my looseleaf. Across the room, Saint raises his hand, and I know what's coming.

"Yes, Señor O'Connor?"

"Señor Faure," Saint says. "You seen those beaches in Spain?"

Faure nods, and the trap is set. It's like one of those nature shows, where some clueless mouse or bird crawls right into the Komodo dragon's path. Right now, Faure is the mouse.

"The Spanish beaches, they are *très* beautiful," Faure says in his accent, which is more French than Spanish.

I fold the sheet of paper in half and slip the photographs inside, not looking at Señor Faure. I used to laugh at O'Connor's jokes. Now, they seem cruel.

"Are the women, like, naked there?" Saint asks.

Faure tugs on his guayabera shirt. "They are topless sometimes, yes."

"Let me ask you, Señor Faure . . . why don't

European women shave their pits? I mean, do they reek?"

The rest of the class is laughing, like I used to when Saint would ask Faure the Spanish word for *copulate* or *mammary*. I sneak a look at Tom. He's not laughing, not listening probably, left hand moving on the page before him. I know he's not doing the workbook. He's doodling. Five years ago, he saw a magazine contest: Draw the Pirate. He's been drawing the pirate ever since. *I think it's supposed to take less than a* thousand *attempts,* I told him once. He just shrugged.

Saint's still going. "How's a guy keep from getting . . . excited around all those topless women? I mean, European men wear those faggy Speedos that don't hide nothing."

I write Tom's name on the package of photographs and pass it to my right.

It's back on my desk before the bell finishes ringing.

"I don't want these," Tom says on his way out the door. But I think I see something in his face, just for a second. Like maybe he's sorry we're not still friends? But he says, "I don't want anything from you, Nick."

"You can't give me a break?" I hold the photographs in front of me before shoving them into my backpack. "We were best friends for, like, ten years."

62

"*Were* being the operative word. That was before what you did to Caitlin." He keeps walking.

I follow him. "You'd think your best friend would give you a second chance."

"I don't even know who you are." He shakes his head. "My best friend, Nick, wouldn't do what you did."

Then he and Saint disappear into the crowd.

Later, in my room, I rescue the photographs from my backpack. The one of Tom and me is crumpled at the corner, but I smooth it as best I can and slip it into my mirror frame next to five pictures of Caitlin and me. I stare at it a long time.

It was stupid thinking I could work things out with Tom. For the first time since Caitlin dumped me, I face facts: I'm on my own.

After Zack's party, I became an addict.

Every year, in an assembly for the perkily named Red Ribbon Week, they pass out pamphlets emblazoned with "Just Say No," spouting the party line: A single joint today, you'll shoot up in an alley the rest of your life. Yeah, right. But being with Cat was like that. My satisfaction seeing her in school gave way to a need to pick her up every morning. Then, drive her home, days I

63

didn't have football practice. Or call after practice. Or drive her home, then call.

For Caitlin's part, she took the locker by mine, a seat on our group's regular bench at Mr. Pizza, and the appropriately named "hump" seat in my car. And we sucked face, lots of it. This was all before I said I loved her, even though I did. I was a junkie. Caitlin was my dealer and my drug of choice.

The one barrier to bliss was Elsa. Elsa was Caitlin's best friend and fellow first soprano (whatever that meant), which translated into my driving her to lunch with us. Every day.

The first time Elsa showed up at my car, I thought I'd picked up a homeless person. She was scrawny, with floppy hat and trailing gauze everywhere. She didn't acknowledge the fact that we'd sat next to one another in English for two weeks. She just looked at me with narrowed eyes, then inspected my backseat like a rodent sniffing for predators. Finally, she said, "Nice car. I suppose you worked overtime at the family farm to afford it? Or are you in Junior Achievement?"

64

I said, neither. It was on loan from my cousin, Guido, who's in the joint. I pronounced it jernt, like in a Joe Pesci movie. Hey, I was joking. But Elsa didn't smile, like she thought as much.

Yet she accepted a seat and rode to lunch with us. Every day.

After three days, I realized Elsa was a permanent guest. I confronted Caitlin before Spanish class, asking her why exactly I had to have lunch with Elsa.

"We've sat together at lunch for ten years. I can't just flake on her."

"Why not?" I was rooting for flakage.

" 'Cause it's something Zack would do, not me."

I told her you don't get to the top of the food chain without eating some bugs. Caitlin fit in with our group, but they didn't let just anyone join their reindeer games.

The rest of the week at Mr. Pizza, Elsa spent the entire hour either talking to Cat or making comments to no one in particular. "I wonder how much that watch cost his parents," she'd say to her sandwich. Or,

"She's trying to prove that less really is more," when Peyton showed off her new crop top. Her hatred for me was obvious and (I won't lie about this) mutual. By the second week, we greeted each other with barely concealed disgust. Before the summer heat had burned off, I'd had enough. Caitlin and I had to talk.

It happened in the Mustang. We'd dropped Elsa off and were going to study at Caitlin's. It was raining. The top was up, and the sound of rain on the ragtop made me horny.

Elsa had been in her usual form, dressed gypsy-style though Halloween was weeks away, and somehow, when we ran for the car, she'd managed to wedge herself between me and Cat, sitting in front of the stick shift. She flipped through the radio stations like she owned the car, finally settling on something by this teen group I detest. I said nothing. I'd rather listen to them than Elsa. But she babbled on, ripping me and my friends. Peyton's too into her boyfriend. Tom's too into his looks. I'm too into Cat (well, that part was true). And the whole time, her mouth got bigger and bigger until finally you couldn't see her face at all. Just mouth. I went in. I reached down her tunnel of a throat, past her intact tonsils, and down until my arm disappeared. I yanked out her still-beating heart and hurled it to the street. It bounced away. Elsa gasped her last, and I switched the radio back to YIOO.

KIDDING.

The music part was true, though. And Elsa's yakking, needless to say. I even got out in the pouring rain to let Elsa out. Once she left, I snapped off the radio. Silence, except the rain, splashing the window, making the world a blur. Like I said, rain makes me horny. I draped my arm across Caitlin's shoulders, fingertips grazing her breasts. Uncharted territory. I waited for Cat to yell stop, but all signals were green, except the traffic light ahead which was—incredible luck—yellow. I skidded to a stop and kissed her, lips moving down her neck. Then, my tongue. A sound escaped her throat. Promising. I reached into her shirt.

"Nick . . . It's too soon." Caitlin pulled my fingers from her shirt and placed them on her shoulder. The car was moving again, and she kissed my cheek.

I told her lots of girls wouldn't think it was too soon, Ashley, for one.

"You want Ashley?" she asked.

I said maybe so. As if. So I said, no. I wanted her. I just thought we were pretty serious. "I sort of thought I was your boyfriend."

She smiled. It was the first time I'd called myself that. But then, she said that didn't mean we were going all the way.

I said, "It's Elsa, right? She hates me, and you think she may have a point."

I passed the turn for Cat's house and got back onto the causeway. Neither of us said anything for a few minutes. The water whizzed by in both windows. Caitlin tried to convince me that Elsa didn't hate me.

Right. "No, she just hates my friends. And my car. And my clothes. And my friends' cars and their clothes. Where does she get off anyway, acting like Little Miss Proletariat? That wasn't a shack I dropped her off at. And if my car's so godawful, why's her butt in it all the time?"

68

We neared the mainland, and I pulled off onto the beach, where people parked nights, in the shadows of downtown Miami. I threw the car into park. "Look, I don't like you hanging out with her."

"What?"

"Get rid of her."

Cat stared at me like I was crazy. Maybe I'd gone too far. For some reason, I remembered her telling Dirk off at Zack's party. But I wasn't Dirk. What I was saying was for her own good. So I continued. "Make your choice, Cat. That bitch or me."

Caitlin touched my shoulder, whispering, "Nicky . . ."

I shrugged her off. "Her or me? Hang with me and all my friends, or sit in the cafeteria with Elsa and her Disney lunch box."

I saw I'd hit a nerve with that one. Caitlin stared at the floor, biting her lip. Did she like being part of my crowd more than she liked me? Was it enough to give up Elsa? It was pouring now, and the skinny pines shook like skeletons by the road. I didn't want Caitlin to call my bluff. I couldn't lose her, but I was protecting myself. Elsa wanted to break us up. I had to know where I stood. A car whizzed by, swamping us in muck. Caitlin gripped the door handle, on the edge of her seat. The rain was deafening. I leaned to kiss the back of her neck.

Her hand snapped back. "Could I still see Elsa when you aren't around?"

I kissed her again. "Sure. But I plan on being around more and more. I want to be together all the time."

Caitlin said she wanted that too. She kissed me and put my hand back where it had been. I tried to continue what I'd started, but my horniness had disappeared. Was I crazy? We were on make-out row, and she was willing now. Too willing. I slipped my fingers between her breasts. No good. I took my hand away. I said, "I've got a test in English tomorrow. I'll take you home."

Her own hand, which had started to negotiate its way across my stomach, stopped. She drew away. We drove back in silence, me wondering at my sanity.

The next morning, when Caitlin opened her locker, she found a bouquet of white roses inside. I grinned as she did a little dance around the hallway. I hadn't asked too much. After all, I loved her. And with Elsa off my back, I relaxed. Caitlin saw her a few more times, but soon, she was too busy with me and with my friends. Especially when she got a bid to join Sphinx, Key's best sorority. They'd never have asked with Elsa clinging like a plantar wart. I knew Cat was excited. All the girls in our group were Sphinxes, and of course, my girlfriend would be part of <u>our group</u>.

The problem was Sphinx took a lot of Cat's time, going to meetings, doing pledge stuff like baking cookies for the members. Once, she had to sing the alma mater, standing on a cafeteria table. Another time, they made her wear the same clothes three days straight. But at least it was with the right people. My people.

Family violence class

Mario's on everyone's case again.

"Does this sound familiar?" he says. "When your girlfriend's been out, do you check her odometer to see how far she went?"

"Don't everyone?" Kelly says.

"How else you know if she's telling the truth?" Tiny asks.

"I'll take that as a *yes* for Tiny and Kelly. Thanks for your candor." Mario scans the room. "Anyone else? Or do you interrogate her about where she's been, listen to her answering machine, call her names, or isolate her from her friends?"

No, no, no, no. I shake my head. None of this applies to me. Or does it? I study the water beads pooling under the A.C. unit and remember about Elsa.

"What if you don't like her friends?" Tiny asks.

"I don't know, Tiny," Mario says. "What if you don't like her friends?"

"Then she ought not to hang with them." When Mario doesn't answer, Tiny continues, cracking his enormous knuckles. "I mean, I don't want Donyelle going around with people got a bad 'tude toward me or our relationship. Her girlfriends all talk trash about a guy, acting like she's all that and could do so much better," he says, and I nod.

"And you don't like that?" Mario says.

"Would you?"

"And what you say goes?" Mario pretends he's confused. "Donyelle has no say? She can't make her own decisions?"

"That ain't what I said."

"Repeat what you said then. I misunderstood."

"Forget it." Tiny flops back in his seat.

"*I* knew what you meant," I mutter.

Mario hears, and I think he's about to challenge me, but this guy named Ray raises his hand. Ray's one of the older guys in class. At least, he's through school. He's sort of serious compared to the rest, which is probably why I figured him for a kiss-ass from day one.

"I understand," he says when Mario calls on him.

"What do you understand, Ray?"

"You're saying it's controlling behavior to separate her from her friends? We shouldn't do that."

Gold star for Ray.

"That's what I'm saying," Mario says, like he knows Ray's a bootlicker too. He turns to me. "I saw you metooing before, Nick. Let's get your input."

"Aww, don't call on him," Kelly interrupts. "Richie Rich is too big to talk to the likes of us."

Everyone looks at me then, so I'm cornered. I hit Kelly with a look. But I decide he's not worth bothering with. Instead, I say, "I agree with Tiny. I mean, should I spend time with people I don't like just because they're her friends?"

"Not necessarily," Mario says. "But can she?"

"We were always together," I say.

"Maybe that was part of the problem." I shrug again, and Mario says, "What about your guy friends? I'll bet they hang with people you may not like. Do you say, 'Hey, Bubba, it's him or me,' or do you just go along?"

I go along, I think, remembering Tom's friendship with Saint O'Connor. I'd spent hours, days of my life with that knuckle dragger. "That's different."

"How so?"

"Because if I told a guy to choose between me and someone else, he'd tell me to screw off."

"Because you have no power over a guy, no control the way you have with a girlfriend?"

"No. 'Cause if you say that to a guy, he'd think you're queer."

"And if you say it to a girl, she'll know you're a control freak."

I look around the room. Everyone's pretending fascination with what Mario's saying because they don't want to talk themselves. Was I a control freak? If I hadn't done stuff like that, would Caitlin still be around? But I go for broke. "So I'll find someone else," I say. "They all have the same thing between their legs."

This gets some chuckles, some raised thumbs. But Mario shakes his head. "Somewhere down the road, Nick, I hope you'll find they don't all have the same thing between their ears. The good ones don't put up with macho mind games."

I'm coming up with a response when a voice interrupts.

"Why don't you leave him alone?"

It's Leo-the-cool. I gape at him, and Mario says, "What?"

"You said no put-downs, didn't you?" Leo says. "That was one of your rules."

"Confronting someone about their beliefs isn't a put-down," Mario says. "Challenging attitudes is the point of this class."

"That's a load of crap," Leo says. "All you do here is play mind games and make people feel stupid."

I've recovered from my shock enough to scowl at Leo. "I don't need you to defend me."

Even so, I'm wondering why he did.

"Sorreee," he says. "Thought you did. Considering you got this look like an ant staring down a can of Black Flag."

"You aren't my mother," I say. But that gets me mad. Why is he calling attention to me when I just want to be ignored? Why is he making me out like I'm some weakling? I feel blood coursing through my wrists, and I stand. I start toward Leo.

But Mario gets between us, real quick. "Are we still in my class?" His eyes are cold. "I know we aren't 'cause there's no fighting in here."

"But he—"

"Not here. You take it to the streets if you have to, but not in my class." He turns to Leo. "Hear that?"

Leo doesn't look at me. "No biggie. I was just trying to help."

Mario turns my way. "Nick?"

"I don't need his help," I say. "I've eaten as much shit as anyone here. He's got no right to act like I can't."

Mario nods. "I agree with you. But fighting's not what this class is about."

"I don't know what the hell it's about," I say.

"It's about God kicking you in the butt so you'll notice the mess you've made." When I look at him, surprised, Mario adds, "Now sit." He waits until I obey, then stares at me until I look away. He turns. "Next session, we'll talk about eating shit. By that, I mean we'll be discussing our families, our parents."

76

He pauses like he knows the reaction he'll get.

Stunned silence. Everyone who's been shuffling around, getting ready to go, stops. He really wants us to talk about our parents? Like, about my *father*? Tiny says, "What's that got to do with anything?"

"I know it'll be painful for some of you—maybe all of us." Mario walks around the circle, scanning our eyes. "But exploring the past brings out the sort of feelings that cause us to become insecure, controlling, even violent." When Mario passes me, I don't look at him. He sits, hands on knees. "Anyone have anything else before we call it quits?"

People start gathering books, keys, backpacks. Kelly's recovered enough to volunteer. "I heard a wicked-ass joke."

"Always got time for humor, *clean* humor," Mario says.

"It's clean." Kelly flips a hand across his hair. "What's the first thing a gal does when she checks out of the battered women's shelter?"

Mario holds up his hand. "I don't think—"

"The dishes, if she knows what's good for her!"

People laugh, but me, I'm wondering what made Leo take my side. And what will I say about my father in class?

77

Later that day

I'm still thinking about my father hours later, instead of doing homework, instead of working on my journal. Fact is, my father is part of this story too. The next part. But I don't want to write about him. And I sure as hell don't want to tell Mario about him. Judge Lehman said she wouldn't read the journal if I didn't want her to. But how can I be sure? Finally, I open the wavy-edged book to a fresh page and write:

(DON'T READ. YOU SAID YOU WOULDN'T.)

Lights blazed on, and I saw the clock. 3:00 A.M. I blinked, tried to cover my face with the sheet, but my father pulled it away.

"What is this?" he yelled, shoving a paper in my face.

I said I didn't know. I stood, then edged away, trying to focus.

But he came closer, screaming, "I will tell you what. A receipt for beer. Beer! Rosa brought beer into this house, so where is it?"

The beer for Zack's party. I said, "I don't know. Honest, Dad—"

"Liar! I asked Rosa. She says you took it."

"She's lying. Dad, I—"

"Thief! I did not raise you a thief, but you are one. When I was your age, I was away from home, working. You only steal from me."

"I didn't—"

He hit me hard in the face, and I stumbled back onto my bed. I lay not moving, not speaking. Arguing made his anger worse, and now I only wanted him to leave. He raged on about how hard he worked, what a lazy ingrate I was, but I stopped listening, my brain carrying me to an alternative reality, where I was watching someone else lying under my black bay window. Then, I went further. I don't know if it was a minute or an hour. I stopped caring whether Rosa heard. I don't even know if he hit me again. My mind took me to Caitlin.

Finally, he left. My cheek throbbed, and I knew I should go downstairs and ice it. Instead, I rolled over and fell asleep to the sound of his footsteps in the hall.

FEBRUARY 9

Parking lot at 7-Eleven

Monday morning, an hour before school, I hold the phone at 7-Eleven, truck exhaust belching in my face, watching a terrier trying to mount a shepherd mix behind the ice machine. Should I call? It's juvenile, I know, calling, then hanging up. But I haven't heard Caitlin's voice in days, only every song on the radio crying her name. Finally, I dig in my pocket for change.

Her number is comfortable under my fingers, a no-brainer. Then, her voice.

"Hello?"

I twist the receiver above my head and take a sip of my Big Gulp Mountain Dew.

"Hello? Is anyone there?"

A group from school pulls in. I've seen them before, but I doubt they know my name. My friends don't hang at 7-Eleven.

"Hello? Hello?"

The line goes dead, and I walk to school, Caitlin's voice still in my head.

That day, lunch hour

I'm actually reduced to eating in the cafeteria. And alone. I try to separate mac-n-cheese with a spork,

80

unable to eat, though I was hungry a minute before. I think of Caitlin. The way she sounded this morning. Hearing Caitlin's voice always helped. . . .

(DON'T READ!)

Friday morning, I stared into the bathroom mirror. My face was roadkill. I brushed my teeth, wincing at the tenderness inside my mouth, the puffy redness of my cheek. I should have iced it. I went to my father's room and stood in the doorway, waiting for him to glance up from what he was doing. When he finally did, I told him he needed to call the school. Somehow, I said, I didn't feel well enough to go. He just nodded. I told him to say I had the flu this time.

He started to say something, but I walked away. Now was the only time I could get away with that. Did he ever feel bad? Never bad enough not to do it again.

I went back to bed and lay there half an hour, forty-five minutes, staring at the ceiling. When I heard the garage door rumble up and down, I texted Caitlin to call me. Then, I waited.

She didn't call back. After five minutes, I texted her again. Then, three more times. Still, no answer. Where was she? Maybe she'd never call back, and I'd just drop off the face of the earth.

I'd drifted back to sleep when the telephone finally rang.

"Where were you?" I answered it.

"It was ten minutes, Nick. I was in class." I heard voices in the background and looked at my watch. She'd waited until passing time to call. Bitch.

"I was worried when you didn't show up this morning," she said.

I apologized for not chauffeuring her to school. "I'm sick, if you care," I said. I knew I sounded pathetic, but I wanted her to be miserable like me, and she didn't sound miserable enough.

She said of course she cared. She'd come over later. I told her no. Because, of course, she couldn't see my face.

"I want to. I don't care if I catch anything."

"No. I said no."

"Fine, Nick. Be that way."

Now, she sounded miserable, but not for the right reason. Because I'd yelled at her, not because she missed me. "You won't go to the game tonight without me?" I asked.

She didn't answer right away, and I told her never mind, sucking my lip. Go right ahead.

"It's just everyone will expect me."

"Go ahead. Have fun with Everyone."

"I won't go, okay?"

"Go."

"I said I wouldn't."

"Go! You bitch."

The background noise had stopped, and I heard Caitlin gulping back tears. Finally, she said, "Don't be mad. I know I sounded selfish, but I thought maybe you'd feel better by tonight. I don't want to go without you."

I didn't answer a second. I was a worm. Because I'd been mean to her. Because of my face and my father's hands. Because I was a worm.

"I'm not mad at you," I said, thinking, I need you. "But I can't go tonight if I don't want to suit up."

"Oh."

"Call me again at lunch?" I struggled not to add please.

Cat called at lunch and after school, begging to come over both times. I wanted her to come. God, did I want her to, but I couldn't let her. Instead, I told her to text me when she got home.

That night, she called during the game. When I asked if she missed it, she said, "I miss you." I didn't believe her, but I fell asleep with the phone in my hand.

Hallway by Mr. Christie's classroom

"Hello."

Caitlin whirls to face me.

I'd be lying if I said I wasn't trying to run into Caitlin. Since I figured out her new class schedule, I've even been bugging out of third period history, hoping to see her. After two weeks, it finally works.

"Nick, you're supposed to leave me alone." She starts to jog toward class.

"You going to have me arrested for talking to you in the hall?" I move closer, and she stops. She carries a wooden hall pass and wears a pink dress, revealing a veil of freckles from days she forgot sunscreen.

"No," she says.

"I forgot my book's all." I rein in the arm that's reaching for her and force my eyes to the floor.

"I know you didn't plan it," she says, her voice uncertain. She thinks of something else. "Did you call Monday? I've been getting hangups."

"What are you saying?"

"I just thought—"

"Caitlin, you hauled me into court, you had some judge order me not to call you." Chuckling at the absurdity of it. She hasn't left. I move two steps closer, the smell of her Finesse shampoo calling up stupid memories of watching reruns together after school. "Throw the order away, Cat."

"I have to go." She doesn't move.

"I'm going to counseling every week. I've changed." I make the big gamble. "You feel the same way you always did, don't you?"

Her face tells me that's true. The hall is dead silent. The big wall clock ticks nine, twenty minutes until the end of class. Her eyes meet mine, and I think I see her hand move toward me. I reach for her.

She flinches. "Don't, Nick."

"Don't what? Who's talking to you?"

"No one."

"Is it Elsa? Saint? They don't know me, Cat." I slide my hand onto her waist, leaning close. She doesn't pull away. "Only you know me. You know I get stressed out, the way things are at home. I never told anyone else, just you. You were the only one who understood."

"I know." I can feel her breath on my face, blood coursing under my hand, the feel and smell of her sending my own blood rushing to all the same nerve endings. We stare at each other, and I see her giving in to the feelings.

Then, she turns away, saying, "I can't take this." She hurries toward her class.

I watch her go. Before she reaches the door, I say, "I never loved you, you know."

She stops a second in the silent hallway. She lifts her chin and stares at me a long time. Finally, she says, "Thanks, Nick." She shakes her head. "Thanks for reminding me why I can't be with you." She slips into her classroom.

I start to walk the other way. Something on the floor catches my eye. Caitlin's pen, dropped in her hurry to escape me. I recognize it from the way she bit the cap. I used to hate that, but now, I pick the pen up and place it in my mouth, caressing her teeth marks with the tip of my tongue.

Later that day

I still have Caitlin's pen when I pick up my journal at night. I've absolutely done my word-count for this week. But now, I just want to think about her, remember what it was like to be with her.

(You're still not reading this, right?)

Twenty-four hours into my paternally imposed exile, the doorbell rang. No way could I answer it. My father, either asleep or gone fishing, didn't stir. Rosa's sneakers squeaked on marble below. I heard her tell whoever it was I wasn't home.

The next voice was Caitlin's. She answered in halting Spanish (she was making a B, but only because I did her homework), "_Él está aquí. El automóvil está aquí._" She'd seen my car. She must have pushed past Rosa, because I heard heels on the stairs, her voice calling my name. I reached for the door then pulled back. I couldn't let her in. "I told you not to come," I said.

Caitlin pounded the door and begged to know why I was acting that way. She rattled the knob, yelling so loud I thought she'd wake my father. Having Caitlin see him, awakened, would be worse than bruises. Out of choices, I cracked the door.

Caitlin pushed it the rest of the way open. It slid over carpet with a hiss. I didn't, couldn't stop her. She started to form her first word, stopped, lips parted, and stared.

I said, "I got creamed in practice Thursday. It's no big deal."

She nodded, almost accepting this. But then, she said, "We studied together Thursday night. It wasn't like this." I told her it swelled more later. But she knew I was lying. "Someone beat you up."

"Not likely."

She stared, and I saw her putting it all together, my absence from school, the fact that I hadn't seen anyone since Thursday, and she took my face in her hand. "Oh, God. Was it your dad?"

I said no, tried to pull away, but she touched my face, moving her hand to the other side. Her fingers were cool, soft, smoothing my hair, and I remembered what she'd told me at Zack's party, about her mother saying she was fat. Could she understand about my father? Finally, I said, "He didn't beat me up. We had an argument. He was drinking."

"And he beat you up. There's no other word for this, Nick."

"He hit me, okay. Once. I can handle it."

"He must have hit you pretty hard to—"

"I can handle it."

She didn't answer. Downstairs, Rosa started the vacuum.

Finally, I said, "No one else knows. Not Tom, not anyone."

"You should tell someone."

"I'm telling you."

"But I mean a teacher or something."

"Tell them what? I'm sixteen years old, and my dad still hits me?" It infuriated me to have to whisper. "I know what they'd say: Butch up, kid. Well, that's what I'm doing."

I'd been wrong to tell her. She couldn't understand. But to my surprise, she embraced me, her face sinking down my chest, and nothing hurt.

"I love you, Caitlin." The words escaped before I could stop them, too late to take back or pretend I was joking. I waited for her to recoil. Or maybe, she'd say she loved me too. Could she? Please say it, Cat. Please.

"I love you too."

Last place I want to be on Valentine's Day

Kelly examines his boot and throws out the challenge. "Say, Tyrone, tell me something. Why do you people always drink orange soda? What's wrong with Coke?"

The members of Mario's group are slumped in their seats. Kelly looks confused, and if I didn't know him, I'd think it was an honest question.

But I do know him. So does Tiny.

"I had about enough of you, Whitetrash!" he yells.

Kelly shrugs. "I'm just stating a fact. Orange turns you people's tongues a funny color."

"Your butt's going to be a funny color you don't zip your lip."

Mario comes in, saying, "What did I tell you about racial slurs, Kelly?" and Kelly shuts up. I slip into the seat by Leo's, but he doesn't acknowledge me. I don't care. All week, I've dreaded what Mario calls "Family Day." I'm planning to say I live with Uncle Henry and Aunt Em and our dog, Toto. Scary thing is, people here would believe me.

Mario consults his class list. "Everyone here?"

"I ain't," Kelly says.

Mario crosses a name from the list, saying, "Xavier's no longer with us."

"Where's X-Man?" Tiny asks, cracking his knuckles.

"County jail for violating his restraining order." Mario shakes his head. "Let that serve as a cautionary tale for you boys."

Mario lets that sink in. Then he pulls a chair up to the circle, turns it backward, and sits. "Today, we'll be talking about families, our parents in particular."

"What's that got to do with anything?" I ask.

"All part of a generational cycle," Mario says. "What happens at home's the cornerstone of your other relationships."

"So if your daddy beats on you, you'll hit your own kids?" Kelly asks. I look at him, and he curls his lip. I turn away.

"Not necessarily," Mario says. "But it's a risk factor you have to understand and deal with." Then, before anyone can use any stall tactics, he says, "Now, who's first?"

Silence, all eyes on Mario. Usually, when he asks a question, someone will jump in, just to get it over with. But knowing one another makes it both easier and harder to talk, and no one's touching this one. Especially after what Mario said about generational cycles. Mario's eyes roll across the circle like a roulette ball. Finally, he stops. He picks his victim.

"Nick, you live at home. What's your family like?"

I shrug, feeling my skin tighten around my forehead. "All right, I guess."

"That's descriptive."

"I try."

"Try harder. Tell me about your father."

"He's my hero," I say, then try to swallow. "A self-made man living the American dream." I'm quoting one of my father's speeches. Next comes the part about how he came from Greece at sixteen and learned English reading the *Miami Herald*.

"What's he do?"

"He's an investment banker. Those are the sharks—the guys who buy the companies in trouble, then sell them off."

"Impressive. He must work hard." Mario walks toward me. "He ever get stressed out?"

"He's fine," I say, squirming. "We get along great."

"What about when he gets mad? Everyone gets mad sometimes. What's he do then?"

"Not much. Yells sometimes. Doesn't everyone?" Around the circle, others nod, except Leo, who stares out the window. Do they know I'm lying?

"A fine relationship." Mario smiles, walking behind me and putting his hands on my chair back. "How's he show he loves you, Nick?"

My stomach tightens, and I remember a long-ago

Dolphins game with some lawyer and the lawyer's son. My father bought me a jersey, even high-fived when the 'Fins scored an overtime field goal. For months after, I'd slept in that shirt. We never went again.

I say to Mario, "We're not into that touchy-feely crap."

"Sorry to hear that," he says, touching my shoulder. "Feels good, sometimes, knowing someone cares." I shrug his hand away. "Make you nervous, talking about your family?" When I don't answer, he says, "No one makes fun of anyone here, Nick. What about your mother?"

I stare ahead. "That's easy. I haven't seen her since I was five." I lean back in my chair. "Someone else should talk now."

Mario nods, and there's another silence. Beside me, Leo's gaze hasn't left the window. Then Kelly breaks the stillness, pointing at me.

"My family's about the same as Rich Boy's, I reckon, 'cept my daddy ain't no Mr. Gotbucks banker." He pulls a sinewy hand through his hair. "He raises me and my sisters though, got a temper, but we get along most of the time."

"And the rest of the time?" I ask before I realize my lips have moved. Are other people's fathers like mine?

"Like I said, he's got a temper. Don't hit us or

nothing. Mostly just put-downs, stuff like that. Don't hurt anyone none."

"Not once you build up that scar tissue," Mario says, and Kelly nods.

"That's about right, I guess."

"Poor babies," Ray, the older guy, says beside me. "Their daddies put them down."

"Watch it, Ray," Mario says. "No personal attacks."

"But that's what's wrong with this country. Right there." He points a finger at Kelly. "Children rule the house because their parents won't raise a hand, just withhold TV or put them in the corner."

"You got it, baby!" Kelly says. "America, love it or leave it. Don't you burn my flag, you commie Cuban!"

Ray says, "I'm from America too, just not your fast-food, Disney World America. My parents came here on a raft. Papa broke his back in the fields, leaving me to be a man from when I was seven. When he was away, I got into two shares of trouble, but when he came back, he whipped us all into shape, including Mama. That's what kids need. Discipline. What I see in this room sickens me."

He stops. Below, the train roars by, and I want to protest the injustice of what Ray said, but I don't. No one does, and I wonder if it's because Ray's life is as familiar to them as to me. No way to tell. Beside me, Leo is silent, but his eyes are dark.

Tiny and A.J. speak now, A.J. saying his father's an all-right guy. His mother's a doormat. To my surprise, Tiny admits being sexually abused by his mother's boyfriend. Through it all, Leo remains motionless, teeth parted, until I wonder if he's sleeping. Finally, he's the only one left. Mario nods at him. Will he refuse? He often does, saying he doesn't have to talk. But now, his black eyes seek Ray, and he speaks like the rest of us aren't here.

"I'm one of those kids you talked about, Policeman." Ray flinches when Leo calls him that, and I know why. Ray never told us what he did. It looks pretty bad for a cop to be in a class like this. "I live in the Grove—the good part, drive a nice car, go to a private school. So I've got it made, according to you. And you're right about one thing, Policeman. No one lays a hand on me."

Ray's eyes could melt glass. Leo doesn't look away.

"You think you know who I am?" Leo demands. "My mother married Hector when I was three, telling us what a good man he was. From the beginning, I heard screaming, lying in bed at night. By the time he started hitting her in front of us, there were two more kids, a Mercedes, and my brother and me at Wentworth Academy.

"Felix and I were twins. He was a few minutes older, but I was bigger, so I was in charge. We shared a room and had a secret language we used in school until they put us in separate classes. Even so, when Felix broke his finger playing ball, my own hand hurt so bad I couldn't write. We weren't identical, though. I look like my mother. Felix had our father's blue eyes."

My mind wanders to Tom, and suddenly, I ache for a brother. Beside me, Leo's still talking.

"Hector had it in for Felix. He used to take me and my half brother and sister to get McDonald's or whatever, but he'd leave Felix home. I'd try to stay home too, but Felix would say, 'Go ahead. I'll just get reamed if you don't.' So I'd bring him back whatever I got, candy or toys from birthday parties. One time, I brought back ice cream. It melted, chocolate all over Hector's leather seats. Hector sprung a leak then, screaming, 'You little bastard! You did this for your shit brother!' He drags me to our room. My brother's making a model car, and Hector says, 'Hit him.'

"'No!' I said. But Hector's by my ear, screaming 'You weakling, you turd! I'll smash him worse if you don't!' and finally, my fist moved without me. I blacked my brother's eye."

"This is such crap!" Ray yells in my ear. "He's making this up as he goes along."

Leo starts toward him, but Mario says, "Simmer down, Ray." He holds up his hand, and when Ray sits, Mario says to Leo, "Go ahead."

Leo sits, and I watch him. "That was when we were nine. After that, Hector knew how to hurt us. Hector wanted me to like him, but I hated him because of Felix. So if Felix did something wrong, Hector made me beat him up. Or sometimes, he made Felix hit me, and he'd scream, 'Don't let him beat you! Fight back, little girl!' Like I was his prize rooster. And finally, I hated Felix because he got me in trouble. I stopped playing with him, stopped bringing things home, wouldn't even talk to him at school. I had my own friends.

"The violence stopped then. Hector had what he wanted. But when we were twelve, Felix swallowed a bottle of pills. My mother took him to the doctor, and they made him puke, sent him home like nothing happened. By then, I hadn't spoken to my twin brother in over a year."

Leo stops, running a hand across dry eyes, and Mario says, "You okay to go on? You don't have to."

"I'm fine," Leo says.

"I don't want to push you," Mario says.

"You aren't," Leo says. "I'm fine." Leo continues, his voice even, like reciting the multiplication table.

"The day Hector and I were supposed to be partners at his father-son picnic at work, I woke up, feeling sicker than I'd ever felt. Ten minutes later, I look out the bathroom window over the driveway. There's a police car outside. The doorbell rings, and I go downstairs, stand behind Mama." Leo jabs a finger at Ray. "She's talking to one of your kind. He tells her my brother's dead, like he was asking for donations to the Police Athletic League. I ran back upstairs. I knew Felix was there. But when I got in our room, his bed was made. Even his bear . . . the brown teddy bear he'd hidden from Hector was sitting on top of his turned-down blue sheet. He made the bed and walked to the train station—that one right there."

Leo gestures toward the window, and we all look out at the elevated train. He pushes his knees forward and rests his elbows on them, looking at us as if he expects us to speak. There's nothing to say. Outside, the train roars by. I watch it, listening to the background music of Leo's voice.

"At the funeral, I saw my mother pretend to cry, her friends pretending to comfort her. The priest prayed God would spare Felix's soul, and people shook their heads because he'd committed such a grievous sin. I hated them. I hated the ones who sympathized, and I hated the ones who judged. Mostly, though, I hated

Felix for being weak. I hoped Father Michael was wrong about his soul being saved."

Leo stands and walks to Ray, eyes burning. Ray looks away.

"So that's how spoiled I am, Policeman. And you're right. My parents never hit me."

We're all silent a moment, hearing the hum of fluorescent lights. Finally, Mario starts to talk, pulling together what we've said, how it affects our other relationships. I want to listen, but I can't stop thinking about Leo's story, even though what Mario says applies to me. Finally, Mario closes his notebook, saying he hopes we'll think about what we discussed. Then, he dismisses us.

I'm almost out the door when I hear Leo say, "Neysa and I have a date tonight. With any luck, this will be my last day here."

"I hope it's not," Mario replies. "That's quite a tale you told. I'd imagine someone with a story like that has a lot of anger stored up."

I turn in time to see Leo smile. "Do I look angry?"

"You *are* angry," Mario says. "Only reason you told that story's 'cause you were angry with Ray. You need this group even if you won't admit it."

"Well, I'll go on needing it," Leo replies, starting to walk away.

Mario stops him. "My uncle Gustavo used to say, 'If you're halfway across the lake, it's just as easy to swim forward as swim back.'"

"Don't say?" Leo turns. "Tell Uncle Gus I hitched a ride to shore."

The following week, Leo isn't there.

Caitlin hadn't been too hot for me to meet her mother, and one look told me why. Tom and I knocked on the McCourts' pink door (which we'd found by walking up the pink walkway, past the pink plastic flamingoes), and before you could say acrylic nail, a woman was on us like an obese kid on the last Twinkie.

While Caitlin tried to ease us out the door, her mother gushed about how she'd been longing to meet us, then demanded, "Which one of you adorable creatures is Nick?"

"Guess that's me," I said. It should have been pretty obvious since I was holding Cat's hand. Caitlin was squeezing the life out of mine.

Cat's mom looked like Cat, but younger. No, really. Her makeup wasn't to hide age.

It was like a whole new face, including painted-in eyelashes. Ripe grapefruit halves peered from a purple crop top while a denim miniskirt exposed tanned legs. A father with a shotgun would have been less threatening. A <u>Doberman</u> would have been less threatening.

No such luck. Mrs. McCourt's eyes dissected me, checking off clothes, watch, Nikes, before smiling. "Caitlin said you were handsome, and she was right."

"Thanks." I think.

Done with me, Mrs. McCourt turned her ample searchlights on Tom.

"And you must be Lacey Carter's boy." She squeezed Tom's biceps. "Your mother and I have spoken extensively about my giving makeovers at the club."

Caitlin said, "We have to go, Mother."

Mrs. McCourt told Caitlin not to embarrass her. She moved still closer to Tom, and Caitlin tried to get between them. Mrs. McCourt gave Tom's arm another squeeze. "Besides, it's not often we have male visitors. Boys haven't exactly been rioting on your front lawn, have they, Caitlin?"

Finally, Tom mumbled something about needing to pick up his date, and we got away. Getting into the car, I noticed something around Caitlin's neck, a silver bead chain with charms, trendy and stupid. I fingered it, leaning across the seat to look.

"Did your mom give you that?" I asked. Her mom was embarrassing, and so was the necklace.

"What's that supposed to mean?"

"Just doesn't look like something you'd wear."

She touched it. "I got it in the Grove with Peyton. I think it's cute."

"You think wrong," I said. "It doesn't go with what you're wearing and it's totally blue-collar. It makes your neck look too short for your body too."

Caitlin didn't move.

"Take it off," I said.

"Nick . . ." Tom's voice from the backseat.

"What?" I slammed my arm down on the backrest and faced him. "What is your particular problem?" I turned back to Caitlin. "I said, take that stupid thing off."

"It's all right, Tom." Caitlin removed the necklace and held it up. "Maybe it doesn't work with this outfit. Peyton chose it."

"Last thing you need is to dress like Peyton," I said.

Cat hung the chain around the stick shift. We drove a block before I plucked it off and threw it out the window. Cheap metal hit pavement with barely a clink. I put my arm around Cat. She moved away.

I pulled her closer. "Don't you want to be close to me? That's what love is all about."

Caitlin didn't respond, but she didn't shy away.

FEBRUARY 23

Hallway behind the Fruitopia machine

The roses are white, veins of green through their petals, a plastic vial of water attached to each stem. I glance over my shoulder then turn the dial on Caitlin's lock. 4-34-0, same as always. It gives way.

In the empty hallway, I study the contents, books crammed in, a card from Liana. A stuffed bear straddles Caitlin's history text. Behind me, something clicks. I turn. Just the clock. It's five minutes into first period. I lay the bouquet across Caitlin's books, close the door soundlessly and set the lock to zero.

Happy birthday, Kittycat.

Later that day

It wasn't like I'd never screwed up with Caitlin before. I had. But before, I'd always been able to get her back. I just had to keep trying.

The evening had been a bad one. Caitlin had barely spoken to me since I threw her necklace out the window. She'd whispered with Liana, laughed at Tom's dumb jokes, and ignored me. I could tell she couldn't wait to get home, but I couldn't take her there. If I took her home now, it would be over for sure. Out of ideas, I dropped Tom and Liana off then pulled into my own driveway. I walked around and threw open Caitlin's door.

She didn't move. "Take me home, Nick. My curfew's—"

"I know when it is. Just stay fifteen minutes, okay?"

Caitlin's eyes searched my face, the car, the deserted street, and I saw anger replaced by resignation. She'd go. I grabbed her hand and pulled her from her seat and down the gravel path before she could change her mind.

The iron gate behind my father's house was painted white each spring, but it was October, and the metal was weathered by sea-spray, heavy with paint-covered rust. I pulled it. The latch creaked open. Our feet met cold, dry sand. I slipped off my shoes and motioned to Caitlin to do the same.

Again, she begged me to take her home. I could hear tears in her voice.

"Fifteen minutes," I repeated. I was lying, but it didn't matter. She'd either

106

forgive me everything or hate me forever. "Please, Caitlin."

Caitlin sighed and threw her sandals by the gate. I tried to take her hand. She pulled it away but followed me down the shelly slope until we reached the shore. There were never many stars there, but the light-bleed from downtown lit our way. I led her to an outcropping of rocks by the seawall, away from the main beach. I pointed at the water and whispered to her to watch. I waited. Ahead was nothing but black water. Caitlin started to look away, but I pointed again.

Finally, a dorsal fin emerged, a bottlenose, a tail flipping through surf. Then another. Two dolphins played in the night ocean. They disappeared and surfaced again. I nudged her. "Worth it?"

She ignored me, staring straight ahead for another few minutes. I was freaking. This was all I could give her, all I had, all I was. If she couldn't understand why I'd brought her here, it was over. Over.

But finally, curiosity took hold, and she said, "How did you know they'd be here?"

I told her they always were. I'd first seen them when I was eight.

I leaned back on the sand, trying to figure out the best way to tell the story so she'd know what it meant. Finally, I said, "I was camping out, lying here almost asleep, when I saw a dark shape behind these rocks. At first, I didn't know what it was. Then, it moved and I saw it was a man. Big guy, maybe six feet tall, hair all around his shoulders. A homeless person, I figured.

"He demanded to know who I was, what I was doing here. I tried to sound brave when I wasn't. I told him my name, and that this was my house.

"He laughed. He said I didn't act like it was my house. In fact, it was his house."

I snuck a look at Caitlin. She was listening, interested. Good.

"He came closer," I said. "His voice sounded rusty, like he hadn't said a word in years. He told me how he'd built the house in 1925. 'You were nowhere to be found, my boy. A Johnny-come-lately, I'd call you. Or an intruder.' He pointed to the water. 'Why,

108

that dolphin's been here longer'n you have.'

"I started to smart off, saying there were no dolphins around, except at the Seaquarium. But before I could finish, one leaped through the air like someone had held up a fish. I stared at it, then him. I asked him how he'd done that.

"He whispered, 'She knows me. Showed up after the big hurricane of '26.'

"He told me his name was Desmond Rodgers. He'd come to Miami in 1925. Before that, he was a Manhattan banker who'd hit it big in the stock market. But his wife, Gabrielle, had tuberculosis. The doctors recommended a warm climate, so he'd moved to Key Biscayne—wilderness, then—and built a mansion by the sea.

"He pointed toward my father's house, and a light appeared in a third-floor bedroom. Probably the maid, but I was eight years old, so I saw ghosts. Meanwhile, the dolphin was hanging in the water like it was listening to the story."

I leaned back, remembering. Caitlin's voice interrupted me.

"I'm not stupid, you know." She drew

away. "I've heard this story before. It's an old legend, so I know it didn't happen to you, Nick."

Nailed. She was right, of course. I was lying. And she didn't understand why. I barely understood myself. I reached for her hand, and she pulled it back. She stood and started to walk away.

"Wait!" I said. "I don't think you're stupid. I just . . . I had to get you to stay. I couldn't let you be mad at me. I had to explain . . . but it's true about this house, the dolphins. I've been watching them all my life."

"Really?" She looked back at me then into the water. Finally, though she tried to hide it, I saw her smile. "I'd heard the story, but I didn't believe it. And I never saw the dolphins before."

"They're here." I edged forward, on my knees before her. "Here, with me. I never told anyone else the story. They wouldn't understand. They'd think I was a wuss."

I realized it was true, not just some line I was handing her to get her back. It was like I'd always wanted the story to be true, and Cat made it so. I said, "Please come back, Caitlin."

She nodded and sat a few inches from me. "Tell me then."

I reached for her waist. She pulled away but let me hold just her fingers. I continued with the story.

Desmond and Gabrielle had lived in the house only nine months. Gabrielle's health was improving, and they thought maybe they'd leave soon. But the storm changed everything.

There was no television those days, no tracking maps with computer animation or weathermen screaming to board up the windows. So when the wind started howling, no one knew what it was. By midnight, coconuts hit the roof, and at one o'clock, some windows broke. But the house was secure. So at two, when the winds calmed and Gabrielle wanted to check on Wotan, their German shepherd, Desmond rolled over and went to sleep.

I paused dramatically at that point and moved nearer to Caitlin. She snuggled close. The dolphins' sound rose and fell. I went on with my story.

The winds began again. The calm had been only the eye of the storm. But the next morning, when Desmond woke, he was alone. He called for Gabrielle. No answer. Finally, he ran onto the beach.

In the yellow light, everything had changed. Palm trees overhung the sand like bridges. There was debris everywhere. No Gabrielle. Desmond saw someone's roof a little ways along the beach. Underneath was Wotan's body. When Desmond looked at the shoreline, he realized his house was the only thing still standing.

I turned to Caitlin. "Desmond walked for hours, calling Gabrielle's name. Nothing. Finally, as night fell, he heard a sound from the sea. He hoped it was Gabrielle. Instead, there was a dolphin jumping in the surf. Strange thing was, there'd never been dolphins near Key Biscayne before. Days later, a reporter photographing damage by the lighthouse found a woman's body washed ashore. It was Gabrielle."

Caitlin slid next to me. My fingers stretched to touch the ends of her hair. My other hand was trapped in hers.

For years, there was just the one dolphin. One dolphin and a lonely old man in his mansion. Then, one day, the old man disappeared. No one ever saw him again. But from that day, there have always been two dolphins in this cove. "My father bought his house from the bank when I was a kid," I told Caitlin. "But I've never brought anyone here to see the dolphins but you."

I stopped talking, feeling a force like invisible hands, pulling me toward Caitlin. I leaned to kiss her. She kissed back, and I knew I was forgiven. We sat, listening to the roar of the surf.

Finally, Caitlin said, "I wasn't mad at you." In response to my yeah, right look, she added, "Well, not mostly. I was freaking about you meeting my mother."

"Why? She's beautiful." I was trying to make Caitlin feel better.

Caitlin twisted her head, maybe to see if I was serious. "That's the problem. Her life revolves around being pretty."

"What do you mean?"

"Just what I said. An eternity putting on makeup, doing her hair. Hours reading

Vogue and even my Seventeen if I don't hide it. And in her free moments, she works on me—all these suggestions about my hair, my makeup, saying I should lose five more pounds. 'I wish I had your youth,' she says. 'I wouldn't waste it like you do.' And I believe her. She was coming on to Tom tonight. He's fifteen, she's forty. I was so embarrassed."

I kissed her again. "Don't be."

"I am. And my father's no better." Remembering she was talking to me, Caitlin backed up. "I mean, he's not like your father. He doesn't hit me. He doesn't have the time to even look at me. My mother says it shouldn't matter as long as his massive monthly support payments keep coming. I know she's right. . . ."

"But you want more?"

"Is that selfish?" When I shook my head, she said, "I'll never get it. He has his new and improved family. I'm just this fat girl he sees at Christmas. Some Christmases."

I whispered, "You're not fat, Caitlin. God, don't you know you're beautiful?"

114

I held her hand to my face, kissing her fingers, taking them, one by one, into my mouth, loving even the taste of salt sand under her fingernails. Caitlin drew closer, and only when she eased her body practically on top of mine did I pull away.

"Screw them," I said. "Think of them as sperm donors, they've done a lot for us, right?"

Caitlin looked at me, stunned. Then, a whisper of a smile crossed her lips. "Right." She put her head on my shoulder. "I love you, Nicky."

I didn't say anything, just stood and sprinted to the seawall. The evening breeze was cool against my face. I jumped, then treaded water. "Come with me!" I yelled to Caitlin, who was still onshore.

"Where?" she said, shocked, but laughing too.

"Key West, Cuba, New York. I don't care!"

Caitlin laughed and yelled that I was crazy. Her mother would kill her, and I said, "Forget her." I started to swim farther out. My jeans slowed my progress, and something else. The thought that she wouldn't follow. Still, I kept going until my legs ached and my eyes stung with salt water. I turned.

Cat yelled for me to wait. Then she was in the water, paddling toward me. I watched her slow progress from shore. When she reached me, she was gasping for breath. I embraced her, kissing her until we both sank beneath the surface. She struggled a moment. When she stopped, I held her there as long as my air held out. Then, seconds longer. Finally, I let go. She surfaced, sputtering and lunged for me. But I was too fast. I swam back to shore with her chasing me. When we reached the rocks, I embraced her again.

"We're two of a kind," I whispered.

"Yeah," she said. "I think I always knew that."

We clung to the rocks and each other until the clouds crossed the sky and kissed the moon. I drove her home, three hours late and soaking wet.

She forgave me that time.

Texaco off Rickenbacker Causeway

It's Saturday afternoon. I'm kicking the curb at Texaco, wondering why Leo hasn't been in class and watching the chimpanzee in his HELLO, MY NAME IS WILLY jumpsuit lube my father's Land Rover, when a familiar car pulls into self-serve. Saint's old white Mercury Cougar. Saint doesn't acknowledge me, but a second later, a girl in a skirt and a pink T-shirt comes out of the mini-mart and runs to where he's pumping gas.

"Missed you," she says.

Saint sets the pump on automatic and musses her hair. Then, he pulls her toward him. "When were we supposed to meet them?"

"An hour ago."

"Then there's no time—?"

Her kiss interrupts his question. I feel her soft lips, her fingers in his hair as though his flesh was mine. "They'll wait," she says.

The pump snaps off, and he walks her to the passenger door. Her eyes follow him to the driver's side, meeting mine in the middle. She looks away.

"'Scuse me, man. How you wanna pay for this?" Willy grins and displays an array of changed-out filters. I hand him my father's Optima card and watch

Saint pull away. My neck prickles from the heat, and my head pounds. I sign the slip Willy shoves at me and somehow drive away.

The girl in Saint's wreck was Caitlin.

My room, ten minutes later

I hate O'Connor. I hate him. Even when we were supposedly friends, he looked for ways to get to me. Being with Cat now is just one more way. I take out my pen—Caitlin's pen with the teeth marks. Funny. Just holding it makes me feel better. And the fury inside me lessens as I begin to write.

Football practice after school. It was the kind of day when your face feels like something's about to explode. Not one cloud in the sky, and the turf reflected heat like asphalt. Saint was our side's quarterback in the scrimmage. Coach Lowery was prepping him to start next year, and I envied his size and gunlike arm. We came from our huddle, and Saint swaggered into position. Dane Ziegler snapped the ball, and I faded left like I was supposed to. Saint ran down the center. The defense bore down. Saint had to pass. He looked right, then left.

His eyes locked onto an open receiver. Me.
Tom came at Saint like a freight train,
and everyone else was covered. There was
no defense in sight. I waited for the ball
to come spiraling through the blue. It
would be a perfect pass. Now, all I had
to do was catch it. I was praying, Please,
please let me catch it this once. Better yet,
don't pass it to me. I'd rather have had
the certainty of not being humiliated than
the possibility of greatness. Still, my legs
carried me toward the end zone. Across the
forty, the thirty-five, the thirty. Saint
raised his arm.

He threw it away.

Lowery's whistle shrilled. Intentional
grounding! Ten yard penalty, loss of down!
His voice boomed over everything, even my
heartbeat. "Shoot, O'Connor, why didn't you
pass to your open receiver?" He jutted a
thumb at me.

O'Connor said he hadn't seen me, and
Lowery tore the whistle from his mouth.
"Does this look like a pacifier? Was I born
yesterday? You was looking right at him,
boy!" Lowery's fists flailed like rudders

for his boat-shaped frame. He knew Saint had taken the penalty rather than risk losing possession if I fumbled. My initial relief vanished. I glanced at Tom to see if he was looking. He turned like he hadn't noticed. God, I'd screwed up without even the chance to screw up. Lowery finished yelling. Practice was over, and I trudged toward the showers.

Lowery's voice followed me. "And you, Andreas. Push in that lip! Be a man for once in your pathetic life."

"Yes, sir." I grinned and moved forward.

Saint walked next to me, smiling. As on the field, he looked me straight in the eye and said, "Sorry, Nick. Didn't see you."

Yeah, right.

O'Connor asked me if Caitlin and I were going to Zack's Thanksgiving weekend. I said I was thinking about it, then slowed to a crawl, until finally he passed. When we got to the locker room, I stripped naked and stepped under the stinging shower spray.

Communal showers are the most bizarre experience in the life of an American male. You're naked, wet, with twenty other naked guys, any one of whom would take a whiz on your feet soon as look at you. The whole time, you're trying to stare at anything except the obvious. Impossible, because deep down, you want to look. Just as a frame of reference, you know. I mean, I knew I was one of the smallest guys on the team, but was I also the <u>smallest</u>? Did height equal size? In other words, was I a runt in more ways than one? And could you even get a fair idea in the shower with the warm water gone? No answers here. I was too afraid of the word <u>queer</u> to look.

Tom stepped out, wringing his hair with both hands. He said we needed to talk. I nodded and started to rinse off.

The reason I'd been considering the subject of height equals size was Caitlin. We'd been going further lately, first in the front, then the backseat of the Mustang. I was pushing for the home run, as Tom called it. It would be my first time, and Cat said she was a virgin too. She said she was scared, but I knew I could talk her into it. Zack had invited the group to spend Thanksgiving at his parents' place in Key

West. I'd make my move then. But could I come through when the time came?

I threw a towel around my waist and headed for my locker. Tom waited, naked as Shaquille O'Neal's head.

The big guy had no qualms about nudity. He stood, staring at the ab "six-pack" he'd worked so hard for. I looked everywhere but down. "Oh Tommy," I said breathily. "We have to stop meeting like this. Those lips! Those eyes! You're feeding my latent homosexual desires."

"More like your inferiority complex, little man." Tom flexed, then took his clothes from his locker. "Hey, I've been meaning to talk to you."

I said we talked a lot. I saw more of him than his parents did. I winced at his still-naked butt. "Much more."

"You think you're funny. Serious, Nick. It's about Caitlin."

"You still don't like her?"

He looked surprised then said, "I like her fine. It's you, Nick."

"What's that mean?"

"You're acting weird."

Suddenly, Tom was all into getting dressed. He pulled on his pants and fished in his locker for shoes. A bunch of other people joined us, and I knew he wouldn't talk now. "Gotta go," I said. "I'm meeting Caitlin by the chorus room."

Tom's voice stopped me. "Well, that explains that."

"What explains what?"

"This is the first practice in two weeks she didn't text you at three-fifteen. It's like she's got a curfew and she's reporting in. Today, she had rehearsal, so you knew where she was."

"Yeah, Tom. Kmart was fresh out of chastity belts."

"It's not funny, Nick, and I'm not the only one who's noticed."

I headed for the door. My clothes felt heavy with wet heat. Saint stood talking to Dane. As I passed, I heard Saint whisper, "He always takes everything so damn personal."

Tom followed me out. "Would you wait? I don't want to get on your case. God, you're my best friend, but you're not acting

123

normal. I mean, that was rotten, throwing her necklace out the window. You call her names too, probably don't know you're doing it, but it's cruel."

"I'm cruel, now? You think I beat her up or something?"

"I didn't say . . ." Tom kicked a stray asphalt pebble. "You don't, do you?" I glared at him until he added, "Nah, I know you don't. But you should act nicer to her."

A crowd headed toward the activities bus. Some were from chorus, but Caitlin wasn't there. Where was she? And with whom? I'd said I'd pick her up, but she should have come out. I turned to Tom.

"Guess we should be like you and Liana?" I said. "What a symbiotic relationship that is. When you have to piss, Liana unzips _her_ pants."

Tom shook his head. "Forget it," he said. "I'll take the bus. You go find your girlfriend."

He jogged toward the chorus group and, in a second, he was one with the crowd.

MARCH 1

Main Highway, Coconut Grove

I am not following Caitlin. I'm not bicycling through Coconut Grove, past the trendy shops on Saturday afternoon, searching for yellow hair among the rickshaws, tourists, and Dalmatians. I can't hear her voice over the birds or the noise spilling from ghetto blasters. And the crowd drinking spiked Slurpees on the balcony at Fat Tuesday doesn't see me seeing her.

Finally, I lose her. Next turn, I'm staring at the steroid-enhanced arm of the law.

"Need some help, son?" the cop asks. Caitlin and Elsa stand on the corner. Elsa smiles and waves. Then a skater blocks my view.

"No, sir." I emphasize the *sir* slightly. Way to deal with cops is give them the respect they think they deserve.

"Might I ask what you're doing here?"

You might. With probable cause. But I shrug. "Waiting for someone."

"These ladies say you're bothering them."

"Don't believe I spoke to them, sir."

His cop eyes meet mine. It feels like an hour. Spots of perspiration appear on his uniform, and I see wheels turning. He knows there's a restraining order, knows

I'm on the same planet as Caitlin. He's trying to put two and two together to make a legal violation so he can haul me off and get out of this heat. It would take a miracle to get me out of this. Then I get one.

Leo steps from behind a line of cars. He holds aviator sunglasses in one hand, fingers in the other, fingers that, incidentally, are attached to this tiny, pretty brunet who's gazing adoringly at him.

"Nick, what it is!" he says, looking from me to the cop and Caitlin, then back at me. He doesn't acknowledge Elsa. "Been waiting long?"

"Long enough," I fake it. "Where were you?"

Mr. Cool smiles and leans against a rack of Spanish newspapers. "Picked Neysa up from a school-related function . . ." (Smile at the cop) "And all the nuns need something done. Tote that barge. Lift that bale—that kinda stuff."

"A Christian martyr," I say. "Don't let it happen again."

The cop looks from the pet store on the right (which sells only Akitas) to the tattoo parlor on the left and, possibly, sees his air-conditioned squad car fade to memory. "You were meeting *here*?"

"I always wanted a dog," Neysa says, straight-faced.

On the corner, Elsa rolls her eyes. Leo must decide the cop needs more convincing. "Hey, you know Ray

DeLeon?" he asks, identifying Ray from our family violence class. "He's with the city police. He's my cousin, knows Nick too. Ask him."

The cop considers. "Well, if you're friends of Ray's."

"Don't forget to say hello to his girlfriend, Diana," I add. Ray would say anything to change the subject away from how he knows us.

The officer strolls to where they're standing. "Sorry, ladies. Can't arrest someone just for being in the Grove."

"He was following us," Elsa whines.

"That's fine." Caitlin grabs Elsa's arm. "Let's go." Elsa protests, but Caitlin's feet are in motion. I watch her go. When the cop leaves too, Leo faces me.

"In a spot of trouble, eh?" he says in his best James Bond impression.

"And you, my truant friend?" I say in the same accent. "Missed you in class today, chap. Last week too."

"Poor, dear Nick." Leo tut-tuts, still British. "That ugly chapter is behind me, my boy." He gestures, by way of explanation, to the brunet. "This is Neysa. We're back together."

"Nice to meet you." She holds out the hand not in Leo's.

I take it. It feels like a warm bird, and I watch

Leo's grip on her other hand tighten until, finally, she releases mine.

"Hot girl," Leo says, his eyes following Caitlin down Main Highway. "Stick with me, I'll help you get her back."

I felt like someone had tightened the lug nuts on my face. Caitlin should have been in the group that came out before. Was she making me wait on purpose? Had she already left? I didn't need this on top of Tom's sermon. I stalked the suddenly empty halls, not exactly sure where the chorus room was, but finding it by the sound of Caitlin's voice.

"Rejoice! Rejoice!"

Why was she singing while I waited? She'd rather sing than be with me now? I turned the doorknob slowly, soundlessly, and slipped through. I stood frozen, watching.

Two figures were by the piano. Caitlin and the guy playing. I knew him. Derek Wayne. We'd pretty much quit calling him "Wayne the Brain" last year. She stood so close, their bodies would touch if she inhaled too much air. Her fingertips grazed his shoulder. She leaned to turn the page, her blond hair brushing his pale face. My fists clenched. She shouldn't touch another guy like that. She continued singing, every high and low note hitting like ice through my eye. Then, in the hardest section, she missed a note. Caitlin collapsed in a fit of giggles onto the piano bench.

"Oh, God. I'll never get this."

Derek stopped playing. "I won't listen to you put yourself down, Caitlin McCourt. You're just fishing for compliments."

"I'm not."

"You know you have the best voice around."

"Oh, sure." But she returned his smile, encouraging him, like she'd take on anyone who'd have her. Slut. They could probably hear my heart by then, so I did the stupid, clichéd thing. I cleared my throat. Cat jumped. Both turned and looked at me.

"Nick," Cat said. "I didn't know you were here."

"Guess not." She thought I was stupid.

She came over and tried to lead me toward Derek. I wouldn't budge.

"You two know each other?" she asked.

Derek eyed me. "We've met." He turned to Caitlin. "I didn't know you and Nick . . . dated?"

"Now you do," I said. Without another word, I pulled Caitlin out the door, and we walked to the car in silence. It was closing in on five, and the parking lot was empty. Caitlin took my hand. I jerked it away. In my mind, I saw her touching Derek's shoulder, her hair against his face. Our footsteps were loud as a marching band in the motionless parking lot. I stopped beside my car. I felt so weak, so used. She was making a fool of me, and I couldn't stop it. Finally, the words built up to the point where they exploded from me. "Why didn't you throw him down and screw him right there?"

Caitlin stopped, backed away. "What?"

"You know what. The way you were coming on to him."

"Are you crazy?" she said. "It was Derek."

The air was thick, heavy. "That's it. I'm crazy. I saw you. I saw you flirting with him, touching him. I saw him looking at you." I raised an arm. It was a gesture. I wasn't going to hit her, was I? But she flinched. I knew I was yelling, but I didn't stop, like that fat, hot air made me yell, made me say, "Slut! I can't let you out of my sight, can I? You can't be trusted, you bitch!"

Caitlin turned to me. "You can trust me. How can you say this?"

"How can I?" Like I didn't know better. "How can you be like that with other guys when you said you loved me? Are you lying about being a virgin? Sweet little Caitlin—you play hard to get with me, but you'd spread your legs for him, wouldn't you?"

I grabbed her arm. The anger inside me was alive, and it made me want things, crazy things. Part of me wanted to hit her. The other part wanted to force her against the car and take what she wouldn't let me have, what I knew she was giving him. I felt every hair on my head, every pore of skin ripping open, and I yelled, "You sleeping with him, Cat? Is that where you learned what we do together—from other guys?"

131

She didn't speak. I gripped her arm harder. "Is it?"

"No." She stared at me, and once she spoke, she kept repeating, "No, no . . ."

Sick of her, I dropped her arm and walked away. "Forget it. I'm leaving."

I got in the car and elbowed the door locked, still not looking at her. I gunned the motor and started to pull out of the parking space.

Then I saw Caitlin.

She stood, crying. No cars in sight. No one to see or hear or care. Caitlin's hair hung in her face, making her look small. She clutched her arm where I'd held it, but I could see a red mark spreading under her hand. I had done that. God, I was like my father, just exactly like him. I had this strange feeling in my brain, like I'd lost something irreplaceable. I pushed it away. Caitlin came to the window. I rolled it down, and her words spewed out in a gush of tears. Looking at her, I felt like crying myself. And I never cried.

"I'm sorry, Nick," she said. "I'm so sorry. I don't know what I did, but I won't do it again. There was no one but you, ever. I never . . . you're the only boy I ever kissed." She knelt to look at me. "Please give me another chance."

She was apologizing. I'd hurt her, and she was sorry. Maybe I hadn't really hurt her. She was worked up, but she'd be okay. I'd make it okay. I opened the door and took her in my arms. "I'm sorry too, Cat. You know I'd never hurt you." I kissed her, first her face, her lips, then her arm where it kept getting redder. I wanted to kiss every hair on her head to keep her with me. "Sometimes, I get crazy. It's just, I'd die if I lost you."

"I won't do it again." Caitlin's tears soaked my face. "I won't do anything to make you mad again."

"It's okay." She was all right. I hadn't hurt her. Nothing had changed. In a way, it felt good, knowing she'd forgive anything. Safe. Still, I wouldn't risk it again. I'd be the perfect boyfriend. Now that I knew she loved me, it would be easy.

I held her until every tear was gone.

MARCH 7

Mario's class

"When is it okay to use violence?" Mario asks at the beginning of class.

As usual, Ray has the kiss-ass answer. "It's never all right," he says, and some guys—truth be told, I'm one of them—start making kissy noises. A few others nod.

"Never?" Mario's left eyebrow heads north. "I was born at night, but not *last* night. We're talking about *you guys*. Do you expect me to believe I worked some sort of voodoo, and you're cured?"

Ray says nothing, but I suggest, "Self-defense?" and just about everyone nods.

Mario nods too. "All right. Someone physically attacks you, you're within your rights fighting back. St. Francis of Assisi would probably buy that. You guys, I've got a feeling, could come up with some other examples."

"How about if someone's attacking an old lady or something?" Kelly asks.

"Grandma's getting stomped, Mr. Steele does a Van Damme on her attacker. Okay. What else?"

Silence.

"I assume no one here's okay with smacking a

woman every so often to show who's boss?" Mario asks. There are snickers, but no takers. "You're sure?" he says. When no one answers, he says, "Good, then we're making progress."

More silence, but Tiny cracks his knuckles like he does when something's bothering him. He doesn't speak, though, until finally we're all watching. "What you think you're looking at?" he demands.

"Something else, Tyrone?" Mario says.

"Yeah. What if she's dissing you?"

"Dissing you how?"

"Like if she say she'll pick you up somewhere, and she's late."

"Been there," I say, thinking about yesterday's journal.

"This happened last week, Tyrone?" Mario says. When Tiny nods, Mario says, "Did Donyelle say what kept her?"

"Maybe."

"You mean you didn't listen?" Tiny scowls, and Mario adds, "You thought you already knew?"

"I knew, I knew."

"What did you know?" Mario asks, patient as an hourglass.

"She was with someone else."

"She was with me," Kelly says.

Tiny stays seated but points a big forefinger in Kelly's direction. "Don't you be messing with me, Whitetrash!"

"Okay, so we've all been there," Mario says. "The woman in your life is supposed to pick you up at four o'clock. Now it's four, and she's not there, and you're thinking"—gesturing toward Tiny—"you're thinking . . . what?"

Tiny blows air out his nose, a sound reminiscent of Moby Dick. "I'm thinking she'd best be there before four-oh-one."

"Okay," Mario says. "But now it's ten after, and it's hot, and you showered after football practice, but there's two wet patches starting on the back of your shirt. She's not there. And you're thinking . . ." Mario glances around. "Nick?"

"I'm thinking she forgot," I say.

"You thinking she forgot? Or you thinking, 'Dammit, that bitch forgot.'"

"Second one," I admit. A few chuckles.

"And why is it the second one?" When I shrug, Mario says, "It's the second because what else are you thinking besides 'she forgot'?" He leans back. "You're thinking she found something better to do? Or some-*one* better? She doesn't care if you melt in this heat because she's never seeing you again?"

"I'm just thinking she forgot," I say. But he's right. I'd probably think all that. I *had* thought all that.

"Why assume she forgot?" Mario turns to the whole group. "How about, next time your girlfriend's late, you think of the thousand reasons that might be— other than forgetting or being with another guy?"

Ray's raising his hand. He's the only one who still does. The rest of us call out when we talk at all. Mario nods at him, and Ray says, "Like what?"

"How about if you thought, 'Poor Donyelle must be caught in traffic' or 'Gosh, I hope Diana hasn't had to take Grandma for a heart-lung transplant' or 'My lord, what if Caitlin's car broke down'? Wouldn't you feel better and—more important—less likely to haul off and smack her, if you thought happy thoughts instead of that same old country song that goes, 'She's a bitch, she's a slut, she's heartless, she don't love me no more'? 'Cause once you start hearing that song, you're in for trouble."

"But those things didn't happen," I say.

"None of it happened," Mario says. "'Til she gets there, it's just conjecture and speculation. Her forgetting is part of a bizarro world you create for yourself. And those other things—the car trouble and the dying grandmother—happen in a happier place. Let's call it Marioland. It's all fiction, and you're the writer, so you

137

may as well write something that calms you down as something that riles you up." We all nod, and Mario takes a clipboard from his desk.

"The reason I mention this is, it's time you guys came up with your personal Violence Policies." Mario's gaze bounces off each of us before returning to his clipboard. "You'll be held to these policies for the rest of this class. But they may be challenged."

"Challenged how?" Kelly asks.

"Held to them how?" I ask at the same time.

Mario grins at us. "I'm getting to that. I want you to take a sheet of paper. On one side, write any situation where you feel it's okay to use violence. On the other, write all the times it's not. Like, 'It's okay to hit someone in self-defense' or 'It's wrong to hit teachers who give me bad grades.'"

"Not so fast on that second one," Kelly says.

Mario ignores him. "Then, if something happens, you only have to check your Violence Policy to know whether it's okay to hit Diana 'cause she left water spots on the glasses." Mario cocks his head toward Ray. "But I warn you, if your Violence Policy says it is, I'll take issue with it, and you'll need to justify it. Otherwise, I keep your policy in an envelope, and no one but you looks at it."

We all start writing. I go with the obvious first,

self-defense or when you meet someone outside after school (which hasn't happened in years), then draw a blank. I turn to the situations where violence is *wrong*. My eyes drop, and I remember the violence behind before I look ahead. I know what Mario wants me to write, that what happened with Caitlin won't happen again. I want to say it, but it seems too easy now that she's gone. And anyway, that's not what I feel like writing. I glance at Mario. "You really won't read these?"

He raises a palm. "Scout's honor."

At the top of the page, I write:

When I have kids, I will never hit them.

I hope that's true.

After class, I step outside. A black Trans Am's waiting, and Leo honks the horn.

"Hey, you got sprung early, huh?" he yells. "Let's go have some fun."

Leo, Neysa, and I head to South Beach, where we spend the rest of the day bodysurfing and looking at supermodels on Rollerblades. When I get home that night, I realize it's the longest I've gone without thinking of Caitlin.

Later that day

But I'm thinking about her now. That's what Judge Debbie said, after all, "Think about what you've

139

done." I am. I'm thinking about it, and writing about it. But what good is it if Caitlin won't even talk to me?

In October, I was the perfect boyfriend. The morning after our fight, I showed up on Caitlin's doorstep with ten teddy bears for her collection. I sent her cards, even wrote a poem once, and peppered her with gifts the rest of the month, ending up with the drama club's Halloween-o-gram carnation sale when I bought fifty, writing a different message on each card so Caitlin was weighed down with flowers like a beauty pageant winner. Me, I got one from Tom, saying,

Do us a favor. Wear a mask this year.

Halloween, we had lunch at Mr. Pizza, as usual. We flocked there days it was too hot for the beach, attracted less by the food than by our ability to take the place over. The restaurant was small, and two of its three benches belonged to our group. The last, we left for whatever losers straggled in.

Waiting by the counter, Peyton asked how I'd voted in that day's homecoming court elections. When I shrugged, Peyton said, "You voted for Caitlin and Liana so you and Tom will get reflected glory from having famous girlfriends."

Did I mention Caitlin was nominated? Needless to say, I wasn't thrilled at her getting that kind of publicity. I wouldn't be good enough for her anymore. Still, I avoided the issue of how I'd voted, telling Peyton, "Caitlin doesn't reflect on me."

"You going to take that from him, Cat?" Peyton asked.

Caitlin smiled. "Oh, he's just talking. Anyway, you and Liana will win."

Peyton patted Caitlin's shoulder and told her it was a big honor for her even to be nominated. Caitlin looked at me for help, but I said nothing. I gripped her arm and steered her to the far side of the room. Then we stopped.

There were people on our bench.

Now, I know it wasn't our bench officially. Still, we had squatters' rights born of two months' staking our claim, and there was plenty of room on the third bench. That's what Peyton was explaining to the intruders. One problem: The invading army consisted of Derek Wayne (dressed as Beethoven or Mozart—one of those) and Elsa (wearing something feathered, which may or may not have been a costume).

Peyton was saying, "But you don't get it, it's our table."

"You're right. I fail to understand," Elsa replied. "Do you have record title, or do you lease monthly?" I figured her comment translated to, "Don't see your name on it," but Peyton was totally confused. Elsa said we were welcome to wait. She turned to Derek, and they high-fived.

But Tom took the seat by Derek. Liana was already sitting, probably the reason behind Tom's swift and wusslike action. I wasn't about to let Caitlin near Elsa or Derek, so after the others sat, I led her toward the center.

Elsa's voice filled the room. "Sit, Caitlin. Gooood girl," and other dog comments. I fed Caitlin a bite of my lunch.

She said, "Not pizza, Nick. I'm on a diet."

"What for? You're skinny." I kissed her. "And beautiful."

142

"I want to stay that way."

But a second later, she snuck a piece of pepperoni.

"Not to worry, Caitlin," Elsa said, not quite aloud. "You can always excuse yourself if you have the urge to purge."

"Ignore her," I said. Derek was staring at us. I fed Caitlin another bite. We crossed arms and ate off each other's forks until Derek looked away and even our friends started throwing balled-up napkins at us. As soon as we finished, I was out of there, Cat in tow. Since just about everyone had come with us, the table cleared.

In my car, Peyton said, "How sad. A lezzie and a geekoid."

Caitlin glanced at me then back at Peyton. Finally, she almost whispered, "Elsa Perez is one of my best friends."

"Yeah, she looked thrilled to see you," I said. "Why don't you hang with her? That's so obviously the cool group."

From the backseat, Tom tried to change the subject, asking if Caitlin was going to Zack's Thanksgiving weekend. I started to say of course we were. It would be our "big weekend." But Cat interrupted, looking at me.

"Actually, I've been meaning to talk to you." Her voice was soft. "I have to visit my dad then."

My hand welded to the gearshift, and I eyed the road. Finally, I said, "Fine. Spend the weekend with the great man. It's been, what? Six months since he called? I'd run before he changes his mind."

"I have to go," she said.

I told her to go ahead. But I wasn't staying home. After all, Key West was a pretty wild town. I hung a right into a space, then got out and slammed the door behind me, finishing with, "You can be replaced!"

I was halfway to school before everyone untangled themselves and Cat ran after me, yelling for me to wait. I kept walking. "Go hang with the geek brigade. You fit right in, you fat loser."

Behind me, Tom started to say something. I ignored him.

Caitlin said, "I'll go with you, okay?"

"You have to visit Daddy."

"I don't want to now." She grabbed at my arm, saying, "I want to be with you."

"I don't know." But I slowed, and she draped herself around my shoulders.

"I want to be with you," she repeated, kissing me.

I kissed her back. "That's my girl." I put my arm around her and slid my hand under her shirt. "I have plans for that weekend, you know."

Caitlin said she knew. Then, she said, "But I'm not sure. I'm afraid."

"Don't be afraid of me." I kissed her. The others caught up by then and followed us, making smoochy noises. I ignored them and focused on Cat, saying, "I'm the only one who cares about you, not your dad, not Elsa. Even these guys are just jealous of you. I'm the only one you can trust."

MARCH 18

Hallway outside Mr. Christie's class

"Hey, Nick! Buddy!"

Saint. We haven't spoken since December, but today, he's behind me. I find my locker and lower my backpack to the ground.

"How come you never told me Caitlin had such a great body?" he says. "Can't appreciate it in those dresses she wears."

He just wants to piss me off, I know. And it's working. I try to concentrate on my combination lock, but my fingers feel thick. I forget the numbers.

"I mean, usually girls who lose weight got tits like little elf-shoes," he continues. "Not Caitlin's. They're gr-rreat." He says it like Tony the Tiger.

Don't react. That's what he wants. But it gets me mad. This guy's a hero and I'm a scum? Around me, lockers slam. I'm still opening mine. Saint's voice rumbles in my ear.

"Mmm, mmm. Much more than a mouthful."

I whirl to face him. He towers over me, licking his lips.

"You wanna hit me, Andreas?" Saint's mouth twists into a smirk. "Be a new experience for you, picking on someone who'd hit back."

He walks away.

After school, I'm at 7-Eleven again, dialing Caitlin's number. She answers on the third ring, and I blurt out, "You know O'Connor's telling everyone about your breasts?"

"Don't call me!" she screams. The line goes dead.

But she listens fifteen minutes later when I call back. I repeat Saint's comment, figuring she'll know what a sleaze she's with. Instead, she says, "Sounds like something you'd say."

"I never talked about your body to other guys."

"No, just to me, putting me down and making me want to die."

"I didn't do that."

"Spare me. You did it all the time."

"I'm sorry. I didn't know I made you feel that way." The sound of her voice puts my heart in my pants again. "We had good times too, though. Remember?"

She doesn't answer.

"How about when we saw the dolphins? Remember that?"

Caitlin doesn't speak, but the pause holds a promise like she's missing me too. Finally, she says, "Of course I remember."

"Does O'Connor ever do anything romantic like that?"

No answer.

"I bet he doesn't. Bet he throws a burger at you and tries to jump you in that clunker of his."

"Nick . . ."

"The dolphins are still there, Cat, and the beach. And us. We could do it all again."

"I can't."

"I miss you, Caitlin. I miss holding you. You know there's no one else." I pull the receiver from my face, hating the feel of someone else's skin oils. I listen, though. Caitlin's breath quickens, and I say, "How about I meet you there in an hour—just to talk?"

It takes her a moment to say, "Make it six o'clock."

"Six o'clock." I hang up, fingering the ring in my pocket. In two hours, it will be back on Caitlin's finger.

Half an hour later

I pull out the journal. I've gotten used to carrying it around, writing in it. But if all goes well, this will be the last time I write. So, today, I'll write about something good. There were those too, you know.

Caitlin was chosen Homecoming Princess. She wore blue and, at halftime, they drove her onto the field in a loaner car from Albritton Cadillac. I sat beside her. Liana

was the other princess, so she and Tom
were with us. We were making the big loop,
and the whole time, I'm remembering the
Kennedy assassination films we saw at the
Smithsonian during last year's Close-up Trip.
Like, one second, they were smiling and
waving. The next, brain city. But Cat turns
to me and says, "This is the best day of
my life."

"Yeah?"

"Yes, and it's because of you."

I reached for her hand, loving her and
unspeakably sad I didn't vote for her. Then,
Liana had to butt in.

"It's not because of him," she said.
"Everyone loves you, Caitlin."

Caitlin said, "They love me because I'm
thin and I'm Nick Andreas's girlfriend.
A year ago, I couldn't have rented space
at your lunch table, and if I'd shown up,
they'd have called me a geekoid or a lezzie
like they call my friends."

"Peyton's such an idiot," Liana said.

"Then we all are, even me." The whole
time Cat talked, she kept smiling a beauty-
queen smile, waving. "Every day since then,

we've practically run to stake out our table so they don't sit there. I do it too."

"That doesn't mean—"

"All I'm saying is it could have been me you were running from."

Liana took Caitlin in her arms. "Oh, _pobrecita_, poor little thing. You're wrong. It could never be you."

"I know what I know," Caitlin said. "It still could be."

We circled at two miles per hour like a buzzard staring down a lunch box full of carrion, and Liana hugged Cat until they looked like a heap of discarded prom dresses. Principal Fernandez's voice came over the loudspeaker:

"And in the red Seville STS from Albritton Cadillac, here come sophomore princesses Liana Castro and Caitlin McCourt with their escorts."

She said it was the best day of her life.

MARCH 18

Beach behind my house

At six-thirty, I'm still waiting for Caitlin. And seven. And seven-thirty. I want to scream at the seagulls to stop screaming or throw myself into the wild surf and never crawl out. And I want to see Caitlin. That bitch. I feel the urge, no, the compulsion to go to her house and make her talk to me. I rise, planning to do it. But Saint's probably there, waiting. I sink to the sand. I'll go some other time.

The sudden rain is a wake-up call, but I don't move. Some of us are meant to be rained on. I lie back and stare at the sky.

March 24

Almost a week since I've written. I had this fantasy that I wouldn't have to write anymore, that I'd get back together with Caitlin and she'd drop the restraining order. Then, I wouldn't have to go to class or write this journal or anything. But that's what it was, a fantasy. The reality is, everything's still a mess. Maybe that's why I don't mind writing about this particular memory. It was probably the best night of *my* life.

After the homecoming game, the girls retreated to a top-secret location for their sorority initiation, and the guys, in time-honored tradition, crashed it. Five of us piled into my car and drove to Jessica Schweitzer's house.

The night was extra dark. My car was filled with the stink of guys fresh from a football game. We pulled off the causeway and into the network of winding side streets. Saint and Zack were arguing about the smell. Zack started out sniffing the air, asking if something had died in the trunk. Finally, he said, "You guys reek."

"We smell like men—wuss!" Saint raised both arms and sniffed his pits. "Just because you're not a player."

Zack said, "I know. It brings tears to my eyes—No, that's your stench doing that." He demanded to know why we hadn't showered after the game. Saint said our post-game aroma was the girls' punishment for blowing us off.

Finally, I pulled over to put the top down. I sympathized. I'd showered at halftime, warmed the bench second half. I wasn't a player either, not in any meaningful sense. When I started the car again, Tom held up two liquor bottles, yelling, "Attitude adjustment hour!" He downed half of one before handing it to Zack. By the time it got to me, it was empty, and Tom was singing his brother's fraternity songs. He got raunchier on the second bottle. Tom didn't usually drink much.

We reached the Schweitzers' street. Everyone shut up except Tom. Stealth was key, so I cut the lights. Tom was giggling; Dane, equally wasted, tried to shut him up. I pulled behind a line of cars. We closed our doors with barely a click and crept across the dark asphalt. Ahead, I saw Zack's silhouette. He dangled an object. I shined my flashlight and saw it was a camera. "In case they're naked," he whispered. We'd all heard about the sorority at U.M. where they danced nude around a campfire.

"We're not that lucky," Saint whispered back.

I laughed, but my body reacted differently, and I was glad it was dark.

We reached the house. Lights flickered in an upstairs window. There was a tall orchid tree beside it. Tom stumbled forward and commanded us to help him up. Dane pulled him away—Tom was too trashed for climbing. And Zack griped about how there could be poisonous caterpillars in the orchid tree. Finally, Saint said, "No guts, no glory," and while the others argued over who was drunker, Saint hoisted himself onto a limb and climbed to the open window.

I shone my flashlight. The tree sagged under Saint's weight. He gave us a thumbs-up, and Zack handed Saint the camera. But Saint climbed down a minute later, saying, "Nick, they're bringing in Caitlin." I climbed up and looked in.

Red candles flickered on the windowsill. The Sphinxes, dressed in black, formed a circle with Caitlin, blindfolded and wearing white, at its center. Finally, Whitney Brockman, the sorority president, stepped from the circle. She started talking about the symbolism of the sphinx and how only the enlightened and pure could know her secrets.

"Some people will have to settle for

enlightened," Ashley whispered. Everyone giggled. Whitney silenced them with a look. She took this way too seriously.

Next, Jessica and Peyton brought soap and water. Jessica held the basin while Peyton washed Caitlin's hands. Whitney talked about how it was the hour for cleansing, physical and spiritual. She commanded each of them to cleanse their minds by telling Caitlin their secrets. "I shall begin."

She reached for a candle, and I ducked under the windowsill, smoke stinging my nose. Whitney paused before speaking again.

"Those weight-loss camps never work, Caitlin," Whitney said. "You'll be fat again by summer."

She passed her candle to Jessica, who said, "Even thin you're ugly."

I'd have thought it would have been something more "spiritual," but apparently, the idea was to unload on Caitlin. One by one, each Sphinx told her what they thought about her—and it was never good. I looked up from the windowsill to see Caitlin's face. Her lips were parted, but she said nothing.

When the candle got to Peyton, she said, "You think you're big 'cause you won Homecoming Princess, but you got picked because the geeks voted for you. You're Queen Geek, aren't you, Caitlin? We only keep you around because of Nick." She passed the candle to Ashley.

"Speaking of Nick . . ." The candlelight glowed wildly against Ashley's auburn hair. "Well, just ask where he got those scratches on his back." The group laughed as she displayed her long, purple nails.

I could tell by Cat's clenching hands that she believed it, all of it. Ashley smirked and passed the candle on. It traveled that wide circle, everyone telling Caitlin how stupid, ugly, and fat she was. Caitlin's eyes were still covered, but her hands worked on her skirt. Her mouth set and contorted. Even her head seemed heavy for her slim body. My own legs felt massive beneath me, like they'd soon fail and force me to earth with them. Around the circle, Ashley and some others smiled. A few fidgeted. None looked at Caitlin. If they had, they couldn't have said what they said.

"We saw your mom last week at Publix." Morgan Davis nudged her friend, Tiffany. "God, Caitlin, tell her to get some normal clothes and act her age. I'd be so embarrassed if I was you."

Tiffany completed the thought. "Really, who does she think she is, Madonna?"

Cat raised a hand to her eyes, shaking. At the same time, something stung my shoulder. Then, my back. I remembered my friends on the ground and looked. Zack and Saint threw pebbles at me.

"Give us a chance," Zack hissed.

I turned back in time to see Caitlin lose it. Whitney extinguished the candle. The room was silent. Whitney embraced Caitlin and smiled, saying, "But no matter what we say . . ."

"We love you anyway," the group chorused. They descended on Caitlin, hugging and kissing her. Peyton and Ashley held her longest. Cat kept crying. I climbed down and told the guys I thought they were coming out.

"Way to hog the seat." Zack gave me a sissy punch. "You didn't even take pictures."

"I'll buy you a Playboy, you little perv."
I punched him back, but hard. He fell to
the ground and looked at me, shocked. Saint
demanded to know what was with me, but
I ignored him. I snuck to the front of
the house, the others following. We peered
around the corner, waiting for the girls.

When they came, the pledges were still
blindfolded, six in all, each led by two
Sphinxes. Caitlin walked between Ashley and
Peyton, her mouth a thin line. Beside them,
Liana stood straighter, almost daring anyone
to screw with her. The Sphinxes deposited
the pledges on the brick doorstep between
two columns. They walked toward a grove
near where we'd hidden the car.

"What do we do?" Saint whispered.
I silenced him with a look, then crept
across the damp, dark grass and stood
in the flower bed. I felt cold sober. The
others followed.

In the porch light's glow, Liana nudged
Caitlin. "That you, _Gatita?_ "
Caitlin sniffled.
"Don't let them get to you." Liana
started to say something else, but Tom

158

clapped his hand over her mouth. I grabbed Caitlin. Tom jerked his hand away. He stared at it, stunned.

"You bit me," he said.

"You stink," Liana said. "And you're drunk."

Tom laughed. "Drunk enough to do this!" He slung Liana across his shoulder and went after a freshman.

By now, they were screaming, but not really screaming. Caitlin didn't scream at all, though. She ripped off her blindfold and smiled at me as we grabbed the other girls and half-dragged, half-carried them toward the car. They'd stopped shrieking except Melissa Bruce, who beat on Saint so bad, he let go. She ran back to the doorstep.

"Stupid," I said to Saint.

"Hey, I'm not _really_ kidnapping anyone."

We ran. Finally, we reached the road's end and stopped. Someone was sitting in the Mustang. I shined the flashlight. Whitney dangled my keys, Jessica sitting next to her.

"Not too bright, leaving these," Whitney said. She rammed them into the ignition and roared down the road. We put the girls down and ran. Liana and Caitlin had their blindfolds off and followed us. The others stood in the dark street until Saint and Zack went back.

After a minute, Tom said he bet they'd just drive around the block. They wouldn't steal my car. I said they'd better not, and we slowed to a walk, singing "The Gang Bang Song" for the entertainment of Jessica's neighbors. When we reached the house, the sphinxes clustered on the doorstep. My car was near the walkway. I found Whitney and demanded my keys.

"No way." Whitney reached for her blouse.

I told her putting them down her bra wouldn't help; it would just make it interesting for me. I grabbed her, and she kicked me in the ankle. My leg buckled. Bitch.

"I don't have them," Whitney said. "They're in the car."

"I can't believe you guys ruined everything," Ashley said.

I walked toward Ashley, glaring. I can

160

freeze people out when I want, look at them
so icy they think it's snowing in Miami. I
wanted to make Ashley shiver. She'd lied
about me to Caitlin. I met her eyes until
she looked away. "Who cares?" I said.
"This initiation's too long."

"It's over now," Whitney said.

"You mean we're not being initiated?"
Melissa squeaked.

"You're in," Whitney said. "You shouldn't
be, but you're in. Thank these guys for
screwing things up."

"You're welcome." Saint laughed like he'd
said something hilarious. "Who's up for the
beach?"

Peyton and Ashley both jumped at that.
The others, especially the new initiates, held
back, watching Whitney until she shrieked
at them to leave.

Everyone started for their cars then,
but Cat headed for Ashley. I grabbed
Caitlin's hand. "I'm taking you home."

"You don't have to," she said.

"I want to."

She squeezed my hand, managing a smile.
With a last glance at Ashley, she walked

back to my car. The keys hung in the
ignition, lucky for Whitney. Tom and Liana
followed, trying to convince us to come to
the beach with them. I waved them off.
I'd seen Caitlin crying, knew how bad she
felt about what they'd said to her. I
helped her into the car, my lips brushing
against her soft hair.

  "You looked ready to leave," I said.
  "It was silly." She edged away, but
I drew her back toward me. "I thought
it would be fun, but it wasn't. I wanted
them to like me. They don't." She turned on
the radio. I reached over and stroked her
fingers. We drove, listening to wind over the
bay and an old Eric Clapton song. Finally,
Caitlin's voice emerged from darkness.
"Nick, do you think—?"

  "No." I remembered her crying. When
she protested that I didn't know what she
was going to say, I said, "I don't think
anything bad about you, Caitlin." I kissed
her fingers in time with the music. Then,
I eased her zipper down and put my hand
under her dress, feeling the smooth flesh
of her back, then lower. She moved away.

I said, "No one's ever made me feel like this."

"Like what? Excited?" Eyeing my straining fly.

"No." I laughed. "I mean, yeah, that too, but any girl can get you off. With you . . ." She gazed at me as I tried to put words together. "It's like I've never done anything wrong."

She leaned over then and touched my cheek. I worked my hand under her pantyhose. The song finished. The next one was fast, and Caitlin snapped off the radio. The road rolled on.

"When's your curfew?" I asked.

"I was supposed to stay over Jessica's."

"Stay with me."

"You mean sleep with you?"

"My father's in the Keys all weekend." My fingers worked up her thigh. A noise escaped her throat, but she tried to hide it. For a minute, she just stared at the road.

Finally, she said, "Yes. I want to."

"Good girl." It was one-thirty. The

breeze off the bay was finally cool, and
I touched her. She leaned back, and I
knew that tonight, the world would change.
She'd be mine forever. Caitlin sighed, and I
stopped thinking, focusing on her skin under
my fingers, her breath in my ear. I pulled
into the driveway.

MARCH 25

English class

Wednesday morning, Higgins, in her turbo teacher transport, rides the geek circuit known as Honors English, handing back American Poetry tests. Cries of the wounded fill the air.

"My parents will kill me!"

"Lucky you. Mine will take away my computer."

Higgins cruises on, oblivious to the carnage. She drops my paper with what, for her, passes for a smile. At least, her waxen red lips gyrate. Maybe. I glance down. A+.

Yesss! The Kid rides again.

My GPA is the only facet of my existence that hasn't nosedived lately. I didn't care much before, but now, I take whatever crumb of happiness I can salvage. Even in American Poetry. I return Higgins's simper with a grinlet of my own. Make her day. Behind me, the whispered grievances continue.

"Like to roll her down the stairs."

"How would we get her upstairs?"

"Details."

Higgins taps her fist on the desk. "Your assignment for the weekend: Write a poem in one of the styles discussed."

Groans. General agitation.

"Does it have to rhyme?" Lucille Shulklapper asks.

"Does it?" Higgins says.

"Other classes just have to memorize the book," Amy says.

"Other classes aren't getting extra points for honors."

Touché.

"The assignment stands, boys and girls," Higgins says. "I expect impressive tales of teen angst, and I expect them no later than Monday morning."

After class, I drift into the hall, trying to imagine a poetry topic that doesn't include Caitlin. I'd sworn her to secrecy about the pages of poetry I wrote for her when we were together. But writing about anything else seems impossible. Seeing Caitlin now doesn't help. Since she flaked on me last week, I've spent every molecule of energy *not* calling her, *not* seeing her, *not* crawling in her window at night, though I yearned to see her, longed for her voice, craved her touch.

Today she's touching Saint. They're doing the between-the-lockers liplock she once did with me. Is she showing off? Trying to make me jealous? It works. My pancreas is gripped by a giant hand. Caitlin and

Saint separate. She heads my way alone. Does she see me? I want to say *I love you, I miss you.*

Instead, I whisper, "Fat pig," and move on.

I'll leave Thanksgiving with Caitlin's mom to your imagination. . . .

After class, Coconut Grove

"I'm worried I'll violate my restraining order."

Mario motions me to sit and I pull a chair up to his desk. I had to wait to talk to him. People aren't clearing out as quickly as they used to; hanging around, instead, to rehash what they've said in class or make plans to meet during the week. No one invites me. I guess I wasn't very friendly at first. If they weren't all so weird, I'd feel left out.

Mario leans across the desk to give me his full attention. "I'm glad you came to talk to me. Recognizing you've got a problem is a big part of solving it."

"Sure," I say, already regretting telling him.

"Tell me about what you're feeling, Nick."

I lean back, taking out my sunglasses. I put them on and stare at him through their dark lenses. "I just want to do something. Like, I have to see her, have to get her back."

"Have you tried anything yet?"

What am I, crazy? I can't tell him about the phone calls or talking to her at school.

"Everything said here is in strictest confidence," he adds.

Yeah, right. "Well," I admit, "I've passed her in the hall a few times at school."

"You didn't talk to her?"

"Not yet."

"But you might?" When I nod, he says, "Tell me, Nick. What is it about Caitlin you miss so much?"

I can't help it. I remember Thanksgiving, Caitlin up to her ears in gravy and mashed potatoes, her mother on the sofa, bitching that we should have gone to Denny's for dinner, me just flattered Caitlin tried to cook for me. But I say, "Hey, a guy has needs."

Mario winces. "We're talking physical needs here?"

"There's another kind?"

"I think so. Lots of times, boys your age will say they miss sex when what they really miss is human contact."

Yeah, that's it. But I say, "No, I think it's sex."

He reaches across the desk and slides my sunglasses off my nose. "Talk to me, Nick."

I blink a second as my eyes get used to light again. Finally, I say, "Yeah, I miss her. You have to make me stop missing her."

Mario smiles. "I can't make you not miss her. I *can* tell you it gets easier every day you stay away."

I look at his fat face, just dying to help me, and I have to bail. "Well, thanks. That's completely helpful." I pluck my sunglasses from his fingers and head for the door.

His voice stops me. "Nick?"

I turn to face him.

"I know you already talked to her."

"How would you know that?"

"From getting to know you in class. You wouldn't come to me unless there was a real problem, unless you'd already stepped over the line. This is serious. Please stay, and let's discuss it." When I shake my head, he walks toward me and takes out a business card. He writes two telephone numbers on it. "This is my home number, and this is my cell. If you need someone, day or night, call me."

I take the card and shove it in my wallet, knowing I'll never use it. I turn to leave again.

Mario stops me again. "I can't make you stay here, Nick, or make you talk to me. But just remember, violating that restraining order is a mistake you'll regret for the rest of your life."

I replace my glasses and walk out the door.

That night, he calls. When I see his name on caller ID, I let the answering machine pick it up. I reach for my journal.

The saying goes that they tipped the country once, and all the weirdos slid to Key West. On Duval Street, Friday after Thanksgiving, I believed it. Two beefy guys held hands in the doorway of a white clapboard building, and ahead of us, a drunken barmaid danced to the music in her head. The real world was across the Seven Mile Bridge, and we were halfway to Cuba, halfway to heaven. One look into Cat's eyes told me which was closer.

We'd finally made it to Key West. Everybody who had to had lied to their parents, and Cat had blown off Thanksgiving with her father. It was worth it. I'd even managed to snag a private bedroom for Cat and me at Zack's parents' place. After the four-hour drive and a day at the beach, we grabbed our fake IDs and hit Duval Street.

Like I said, it was crowded. Outside a T-shirt shop, a dirt-crusted guy in stringy shorts played guitar for tips. Liana's hips gyrated to the music. Tom looked at the sidewalk. Zack kicked the guy's guitar case closed. The guy didn't look up, just stopped playing and reopened it.

I kicked it again.

"Quit it," Saint said. "Guy's trying to earn a living." He pulled a five from his wallet and threw it into the case. What a philanthropist.

The guy stopped playing, eyeing the five. Then he put down his guitar, stood, and threw his arms around Saint's neck, saying, "God bless you, man!"

We all stared. "I think he slipped O'Connor the tongue," Zack whispered.

Saint finally broke free. Three doors down, he said, "Shit, I was going to ask for change."

"I can't believe you let him touch you," Peyton said.

"What should I have done? Punched him out?"

"Ignored him like everyone else," Peyton said.

"I think it was nice," Caitlin said to Saint, taking his side, as usual. "Helping a fellow human being."

"A fellow human being with fleas," I said.

"What a snob," Saint said. Liana and Caitlin nodded.

"You're just a better person, I guess," I said. It bugged me, Caitlin sucking up to O'Connor.

Tom said nothing. He looked first at me, then Liana, like he was scoring a tennis match. Finally, he pointed to Liana's guidebook. "We should see Hemingway's house. It says here some of his cats have extra toes."

We laughed then and moved through the tequila-powered crowd. Cat spotted a teddy bear in a window and looked to me for permission to stop. I told her no way was she carrying that crap around. Instead, we ducked into a bar, one with no name above the door but live music pouring out. They didn't even check ID. Two guys onstage were finishing a song when we arrived. The pudgy guitar player started another, the shoeless harmonica player joining in, although his missing teeth must have made it hard to play. Some older people danced to music that wasn't meant for dancing. I said it looked beat.

"I think it's colorful," Caitlin said. Was she going to contradict everything I said?

"Who asked what you thought?" I said. But the others went for beer, and I followed. The song finished. I played pool with Ashley standing close by. I had a second beer, and Tom emptied two bowls of peanuts. I'd been buzzed earlier. By then, I was flying. I ignored Cat and circled the pool table with Tom.

"Don't get drunk," he said to me. "We're snorkeling tomorrow."

"Mom? That you? It's been a while. Your little boy's done growed up."

That shut Tom up pretty fast.

Two beers later, I noticed Cat talking to Zack. They looked pretty cozy actually, considering she'd always said she hated him. I guess hosting us meant he got a chance at _my_ girlfriend. Now she sat at his table, and he leaned close to whisper in her ear. I walked over.

"Isn't Caitlin beautiful?" I said, placing my hands on her shoulders. I had to repeat it, yelling over the guitar feedback, but finally Zack agreed that, yes, Caitlin was beautiful. I said, "Almost makes you forget how fat and ugly she was a few months ago."

174

Everyone heard that. Everyone heard because the song ended, and I was still yelling. Heads turned, first to me, then Caitlin.

"Come on, Cat," I said. "Show them how hot you look. You know you want everyone to see." I grabbed her hand and yanked her forward. She wore a shirt over a white tank top. I tugged at the shirt. "Show them your tits, Cat."

"Stop it!" She pulled away and dove for the chair.

I blocked her way. "Come on. I want everyone to see what I'm getting."

"This is because you're drunk," she said, sitting.

I yanked her up. "Don't you ever sit when I say stand." I pulled her toward me even as she struggled to escape. By then, everyone was staring. Tom was behind me, trying to make me shut up. Someone yelled at me to leave Caitlin alone.

"Hey, why aren't you rednecks playing?" I yelled.

"Waiting for you to let go of the lady," the toothless one said.

"Make me. I'll knock out your other tooth." I kissed Caitlin hard. "She's with me."

"Hey, how old are you anyway, boy? This ain't no day care center."

They were playing "Friends in Low Places" when the manager threw us out.

Leo's house on Bayshore Drive, Coconut Grove

"Everyone knew you were lying that day."

Leo throws the accusation like a practice pitch in the Marlins game we're watching. It's the fourth Sunday in a row I've spent in Leo's undecorated room, watching a sporting event I mostly don't care about. I'm comfortable here, though. I'd always watched sports with Tom, but with Leo, there's a bond Tom and I didn't have. Leo and I both grew up in hell.

Still, I ignore his statement. On-screen, a runner slides home. The umpire calls him out.

"He was so safe!" I yell.

"Nah—he was out," Leo says.

"You see as well as the umpire," I say. "They need instant replays."

"And that's your expert opinion?" He laughs.

I point to my fist, but I laugh too, and we go back to watching the game. The next player strikes out. Finally, Leo says, "Did you hear me?"

"What day?" I ask too quickly.

"Earth to Nick." Leo leans near my ear. "I mean that day Mario asked about your old man." Leo's eyes never leave the screen. Like Tom, Leo's an athlete who considers watching the game homework. He told me he's had college and even pro scouts at his baseball games. "You were so full of it, acting like you and your dad were buddies."

I don't answer, staring at the game and thinking about my poem for English class. Finally, I change the subject. "Where's Neysa? She's usually around."

Leo's dark eyes swerve toward me. "Some family event that doesn't include me. Bitch."

"You want to do stuff with her family?"

"'Course not. But why does she have to? I told her she'd better start thinking about what I want, not just people who try to break us up."

I hear Mario's voice in my ear, talking about controlling behavior. I shake it off. Leo's not controlling. He's like me. He's just looking out for his relationship. On-screen, there's the typical SUV ad, a red truck on muddy mountains. I wonder if Caitlin's with Saint right now.

Leo interrupts my thoughts. "I'm not talking about Neysa. I'm talking about you. We've been hanging together a month now, and it bugs me."

"Huh?"

"I spilled my guts in class, but your guts—" He makes a slicing motion across his stomach. "Your guts are intact. You got off easy."

"Easy? I'm doing time every Saturday. How'd you manage that, if you don't mind my asking?"

Leo rubs thumb and fingers together in the classic "payoff" gesture. "Hector talked to Neysa's parents, and they decided to come clean. Her cousin's the one who roughed her up."

"They dropped the charges?"

"No sense jeopardizing my future for a case of mistaken identity."

He looks to me for confirmation, and I nod. But I'm thinking, *God, he paid them off.*

"So, answer my question."

Cornered, I say, "The answer is, you know the answer. Sure, my dad and I don't get along. No big story. He knocks me around sometimes, not as much lately." Leo nods, not prodding me to go on, so I do. "I deal with him like you deal with Hector. I steer clear of him."

Leo throws me a look then holds it, a dealer weighing cocaine with his eyes. I must pass inspection because he says, "Know how I deal with Hector?" When I shake my head, he walks to the closet and opens its white louvered door. Inside, there are baseball cleats, rows of hanging pants. A safe. Leo kneels, turns the knob. The door swings open. He reaches inside.

He takes out a gun.

He holds it toward me. It is small and gray. From the care Leo takes handling it, I understand it's also loaded. I hesitate, then my fingers close around its smooth metal barrel. The rest of it looks well-used. Though it weighs barely more than one of Caitlin's hand weights, my arm sinks with the heft of it.

"It's real?" Stupid question.

Leo raises an eyebrow. "What do you think?"

On television, the sportscaster screams, but it seems a whisper. The pitches come closer together, and every crack of the bat is a gunshot.

"You'd . . . use it?"

"If I have to." Leo takes the gun back. "I won't, though. Hector knows I have it, knows it's loaded, ready to go, and if he hurts any of us . . ." Leo raises the weapon like one used to handling such machinery and aims for the wall. "Boom."

He returns it to the safe, goes back to watching the game. But a few minutes later, he says, "You can borrow it, anytime."

Later that day, around 7:00

Writing in this journal seems better than thinking about what Leo showed me this afternoon. And a lot better than writing a poem for Higgins's class.

180

Saturday was the day we saw the shark.

By nine the next morning, we'd sobered up (not counting the three coolers we'd loaded onto Zack's parents' yacht) and were bound for a reef off Key Largo. Zack drove like a wild man, and I loved watching Caitlin's body as the boat bounced across the waves.

Caitlin was terrified. In case you think I'm exaggerating, I'll clarify. Caitlin was scared of water, boats, snorkeling, and sharks, stingrays, sawfish, and barracuda. That day, she was probably also afraid of tuna, suntan lotion, and Diet Coke. I tried to help by telling her that if we saw a great white, I'd stick my leg in his mouth—so she could swim to safety.

"You're not very funny," she said. But I thought I saw her lips crinkle upward, so I kept going, telling her how sharks can swim eleven miles per hour. Even an Olympic swimmer can only do five.

I bent my leg backward. "Would you love me if I only had a stump?"

That got her. She cracked up. Between giggles, she said, "Let's avoid the issue by staying on the boat."

But Zack was dropping anchor, and the others were already sliding to join the early arrivals at the reef. Tom yelled for us to join them. I waved him off.

"You don't have to, Caitlin," I said. "But even if something happened, you'd die in this magical place with the person who loves you most in the world."

"You're not afraid of dying?"

"No one's dying." When she kept looking at me, I said, "No, I'm not afraid of that."

She touched my shoulder. "What are you afraid of?"

"Being without you," I answered, before thinking.

She kissed me. "You aren't afraid of anything, then." She looked at our friends and reached for her fins. After putting them on, she started to pull off the Hard Rock Cafe T-shirt she'd worn over her bathing suit. I stopped her.

"Keep it on. You'll fry otherwise."

"I have on sunscreen."

I eyed Liana's butt in the water, imagining people looking at Caitlin like that. I didn't want anyone looking at her like that. "Look, I didn't want to say anything, but you've been eating like a pig lately, and it shows."

She examined her stomach. "You think so?"

"I'm the only one who'll tell you the truth."

It worked. Caitlin sighed, slipped her swim vest over the T-shirt, added mask and snorkel. Then, as if she'd decided to get it over with, she jumped in. I watched the ocean filtering through her fingers, the trail of her yellow hair. Cat had courage stored for the winter. I loved and hated that, hated it because I wanted her to need me. She had to need me. Still, I followed in her wake. Though she'd said she wasn't a strong swimmer, Caitlin pushed on. I only hoped she'd take me with her.

Underwater was gray and bright at the same time. Breathing through a snorkel, all you can hear is your own snorkel-enhanced breath in your ears. But there was plenty to see. First, there was the reef, surprising shades of purple, green, and gold with small fish who let us be part of their schools.

Other creatures materialized. If anyone saw something worth investigating in the folds of coral, we'd take deep breaths and skim down far as our air would hold us. Down there, that seems like forever. Breathing was unimportant. We made a game, seeing who could find the best sights to show the rest. At first, there were only the usual clown and parrot fish, floating like forgotten balloons. Soon, I spotted a huge 'cuda in the shadow of someone's boat. I was Lord High Ruler, at least until Saint said he saw a sawfish. Funny thing was, no one else could find this enormous thing. Saint insisted it was in the rocks somewhere.

"It's in your mind," I said, and he gave me the finger.

We wasted ten minutes searching for a nonexistent sawfish and were starting to think about lunch. Then, Liana surfaced with bright eyes and one word. "Shark."

Cat started paddling toward the boat. I yelled, "Eleven miles per hour, Cat!"

Liana glared at me. "It's a nurse shark. They're harmless." She swam after Caitlin.

"She doesn't have to go." I followed

them while everyone else dove down to investigate. Caitlin hung with one foot on the boat's ladder.

"Don't scare her, Nick," Liana said. Then, to Caitlin. "It won't hurt you, Gatita. Come and see."

"I'm not the one pushing her," I said.

"Oh, right. Mr. Patient and Understanding. You forget, I know you, Nick."

Liana joined Caitlin where she hung. Around us, heads popped through blue water, everyone talking about how cool the shark was.

"Come on, Cat," Liana said. "Let's go together."

"I said, don't push her," I said.

"Butt out."

"I'll go," Caitlin said. "I'll go, okay?"

Liana extended her hand, and before I could join them, they were under. I spit out my snorkel and followed, down, down, past the living purple coral to the gray world below. The shark was still there, barely visible, lurking huge and silent within an outcropping of rocks. I saw eyes, beady and close, nose like a dog's snout. Though it could have killed us with one swift chomp, it only floated, bright round eyes meeting mine. Caitlin hung back. She and the shark watched each other. Finally, she realized it wasn't going to jump out like an amusement park monster, and she swam closer.

We were down there ten seconds, maybe. Liana left, and I started to feel my lungs give out. I was gulping to make myself feel like I had air, exhaling like crazy. Unable to last longer, I grabbed Cat's hand, and we swam for the surface. My lungs felt thick. Caitlin came up an instant later.

"I did it," she said, like a kid who'd eaten a bug on a dare. "I can't believe it. Wasn't she beautiful, Nicky? I just know she was a girl shark. And I wasn't afraid. Me. I wasn't afraid. Can we go again?"

Cat was practically panting, but her eyes shone. I looked up at the boat. "I don't know. We've been in over an hour. Everyone's having lunch."

She didn't argue, just said, "Oh, well. At least, I saw her," and swam toward the boat. She threw off her flippers and ran to Liana, thanking her for making her go. I was forgotten.

"You did it, Gatita." Liana snuck a glance at me. "I just believed in you."

After lunch, sandwiches prepped by the Schaeffers' maid, we settled in. I'd oiled up and insinuated my body next to Cat's, balling a towel over my trunks in anticipation of the borderline sick sex dreams that come from sleeping in sun. I closed my eyes, waiting for sleep to take me. I felt a tap on my shoulder.

I pulled an eye open. It was Tom. "'sup, bruthuh?"

He put a finger to lips and gestured toward Saint, who looked like a beached rhinoceros on his stomach. Tom crept toward him and whispered something in his ear. No response. Tom whipped out a zinc oxide stick and started writing. When he finished, he stood back so I could see. I laughed. He'd inscribed JUSTIN 4EVER! in zinc on O'Connor's unsuspecting back, assuring Saint a semipermanent skin shrine to the god of tween-age girls. O'Connor would not be a

187

happy camper when he woke up.

I said no way was I sleeping now, but Tom said, "Don't worry. Next one's for me." Tom flopped on a towel and started drawing on his leg with zinc. No one stirred. Pretty soon, Tom the artiste had drawn a creditable dolphin, the school mascot.

"Do you do Billy the Marlin too?" I asked.

Tom laughed. "For a price."

"What price?"

"Information. Noticed you and . . ."—he gestured toward Caitlin— "shared a room last night. Bed too, I'd imagine. You doing her?"

Cornered, I grinned. "I prefer to think of it as the ultimate physical expression of our spiritual oneness."

"Which involves what—doing her?"

"If you want to be gross."

"And proud of it." Tom slapped my shoulder, letting me know I needed more lotion. "I can't believe you didn't tell me."

"You didn't tell me your first time."

"One good reason." Tom looked around then lowered his voice. "I am pure as a newborn babe."

188

"You're shitting me."

"I shit you not. Liana's saving herself for marriage."

"Think Cat wasn't?"

Tom leaned on his elbow. "You didn't . . . force Caitlin or anything?"

"'Course not. Just let her know she wasn't the only girl around." I reached for Tom's Panama Jack, glancing at Caitlin. Her eyes were closed, her face motionless. "You can't be so whipped. You have to call the shots."

Tom sat up. "I just heard that. Who you calling whipped?"

"A guy who's whipped."

Tom was on me. I put up a fight, yelling, "You trying to get some from me because you can't get it anywhere else?" No one stirred. We fought harder, like we used to fight when we were kids. He pinned my arms. He was laughing, but I could tell he was a little serious too.

"Am I still whipped?" he yelled.

"Like cream. Which incidentally is—"

I didn't finish. He pulled me up and dragged me to the side of the boat. "Still?"

I nodded.

He hoisted me onto the rail. I kicked him a few times before I stopped struggling and grinned at him.

"You know, this is interesting," I said. "I read somewhere that purity brings superhuman strength."

"Asshole!" Tom pushed me into the ocean.

I fell, head-on, and got a throatful of salt water. When I surfaced, spitting out the ocean, my first words were, "Still whipped."

Tom jumped almost on top of me with a splash that should have awakened everyone. We both treaded water a minute. He said, "You know, I'm glad you were first. You had so much more to prove."

10:30 P.M.—my desk, third straight hour

Teammates

Whistles shrill high, let the skirmish begin.
Bodies colliding, sun stings my naked eyeballs.
Feinting, then attacking, they struggle to win,
But I'm on the sidelines apart from the crowd.

Your eyes meet mine and see only reflection.
Your legs piston, powerful, a hero once more;
And I stand alone, drenched in sweat and untold secrets;
But slapping your hand, saying everything's fine.

I stare at the lines my hands, apparently incommunicado with my brain, have typed. I'm screwed if I turn this in. Football seemed like a safe topic. I chose blank verse because my mind was equally blank. At least, I thought it was. But I ended up writing, about Tom, things I hadn't even thought I'd thought.

An hour later, the poem's still in my face. My brain is an abyss. I try, but the only images I can channel are of Caitlin. Caitlin dancing on Duval Street, Caitlin's hands fanning green waters, Caitlin swimming in the moonlight. I blame the journal. It's become my torment and my salvation, the cable that binds me to the past by being my sole reality. And somehow, when I see it on paper, it becomes more real than when it's just in my head. I should stop writing. Mario doesn't look at it, and it makes me think pointless thoughts, wonder if things could have been different. With Cat? With Tom even? If I'd told Tom how it was at home, would it have changed anything? He was my best friend. Could he have helped?

No. He'd have laughed at me.

I shove the poem into my backpack and take out my journal. I'm back with Caitlin. Except I don't want to be where I'm going now.

The road north was straight and long. The mangroves surrounding it stank like stale beer. Cat and I were alone, me memorizing the license number ahead, an out-of-state tag that said FISHIN, Caitlin wearing sunglasses, eyeing the five o'clock sky. Why was she so relaxed? She wasn't stuck driving, that's why, wasn't driving down this two-lane road behind FISHIN, who traveled below the speed limit. Jesus Christ. I sped up, almost tapping his bumper. Cat opened her mouth and shut it. Good choice.

One-word signs lined the road:

> PATIENCE
>
> PAYS
>
> ONLY
>
> TWO
>
> MILES
>
> TO
>
> PASSING
>
> ZONE.

I had no patience. Two miles took five minutes because of FISHIN. Finally we hit the passing zone, and I gunned past five cars, barely slipping in front of the last. We were near the Seven Mile Bridge. I could see water ahead. Caitlin stirred beside me, fiddling with her sunglasses.

Finally, she said, "Nick, we need to talk."

"About what?"

She moved away. "About Friday on Duval street. How you were drinking, how you acted."

I clutched the wheel. Friday was pretty much a blur, although Tom and Dane had reamed me for getting us thrown out of that bar. "How I acted?"

"Nick . . . you know I love you."

"But?"

"Sometimes, you act like someone else."
Caitlin looked away. I stared forward, but
my heart was ramming into my ribs. Did she
want to break up? "Sometimes you're not
nice to me," she concluded.

"Not nice, huh?" I said. She could not
leave me. Cat turned toward the window.

"Sometimes, it's like you don't trust
me," she said.

She _was_ trying to break up. Who was
it? Saint? Maybe even Zack? My tires met
the bridge, two lanes suspended between
sky and water. The ultimate no-passing zone.
Only an occasional car drove the left lane,
but visibility sucked. Sun turned water
tangerine. Caitlin fidgeted.

"I said you don't trust me."

"I heard you. I'm deciding how to
respond." She could not leave me. As I
hit the word _respond_, I pulled to the left,
veering into the southbound lane. Then, I
floored it past three cars. A southbound
Volvo station wagon slammed its brakes

194

within yards of us. The driver was honking, yelling. I pulled back into the northbound lane and flipped him off. I looked at Caitlin. Her mouth hung in midscream. I laughed.

"Do you trust me, Cat?" She was silent. I leaned closer. "Did I ever tell you about my mother?" Caitlin recovered enough to shake her head no, and I said, "I was four, five, I'd lie awake nights, listening to her and my dad fighting, him hitting her." I looked at Caitlin. "You want to hear this?"

She nodded.

"I thought we'd pack up and leave someday, her and I. I lived for that day." On the wheel, my knuckles were white. "Then, one morning, I wake up, and she's gone, never came back. She ran from the monster and left me there with him."

Caitlin removed her sunglasses. "I'm sorry, Nick."

"So you talk about trust, it's pretty important. I mean, when the one person you trust just picks up and leaves . . ."

Caitlin's hand slipped across my shoulder. I tried to shrug her off, swerving left into traffic, then back. Terror filled Caitlin's eyes. Her nails ripped my flesh.

"Trust me, Cat?" She could not leave me. I swerved again. "'Cause if you haven't figured it out, life doesn't mean much to me. Without you, it's worthless."

A flock of seagulls headed across my windshield. She could not leave me. I swerved again, this time counting three before I veered back. She could not leave me. Caitlin screamed at me to stop.

"What's the matter?" When she didn't answer, I swerved again. "Oh—this. Maybe you're right."

I straightened the wheel, looking beyond her to the orange and green water east of the bridge. Silence. I didn't swerve. Nothing. We were halfway across. Caitlin relaxed.

Suddenly, I said, "Think I could make a right here?" Right was into water. I made like I'd do it, crash through the guardrail, then down. Caitlin screamed. She grabbed for the wheel. I shoved her away so her fingers clawed the air. She tried again, gripping both my hands. The car swerved left into the path of a Bronco towing a boat. I pulled it back. My mind knew what she was doing, but my eyes didn't. I couldn't see her. She was shrieking. God, shut up! Her voice deafened me, and it was all around, in my ears, making me lose all control. She tried to grab the wheel. Blind and deaf, I drove, sun hot on my face. I had to get her off me. God, I just had to get her off me. Get her off me! Get off me! Get off!

Next thing I knew, I was driving on land. I couldn't tell you whether it was minutes or hours later. Caitlin hung across the seat, head cradled in her fingers. My hand throbbed, and I knew I'd hit her. I'd hit her. I was tired. She'd worn me out, but the anger inside me dissolved, replaced by that regret. But I'd had to stop her. She'd been irrational, overwrought, shouldn't have touched the wheel. She could have killed us. I looked at her. The seat was the length of a football field. Caitlin faced the window. She was so beautiful. Ahead was a red pickup with a Jesus fish. It was going at a good clip, but when we reached the next passing zone, I overtook

it and a few other cars. Cat stiffened. I
merged back into traffic and reached to
stroke her hair.

She lifted her head, cautious as a
runner stealing home, and stared.

"Are you all right, Caitlin?" I asked.

When she didn't answer, I repeated the
question.

She shook her head. "You hit me."

I told her no. I hadn't. I mean, she was
grabbing the wheel. We'd almost creamed the
Bronco. I had to get her off me before we
got killed.

"Because you were driving off the
bridge," she said.

I laughed and said she knew me better.
I was just screwing around, like when we
kidnapped them from Jessica's. I'd never
do it for real. Besides, we'd have crashed
the guardrail, and I'd have gotten killed for
wrecking the car.

"But you hit me, Nick." She leaned out
the window toward the sideview mirror to
see if her cheek was getting red.

And it was. I didn't expect it to be
red, but it was—a little. I hadn't hit her

198

hard, just enough to get her off me. I said,
"Don't you know you shouldn't grab the
wheel when someone's driving?"

"But I thought—"

She was pretty shaken. Mad maybe? I
pulled her close. "Sorry I freaked you out,
Kittycat. I forget you aren't used to guys.
You don't know we play rough sometimes."
She kept protesting, and I said, "You know
what I was thinking? I wanted to buy you
a ring. You know, like a symbol, since we're
going together. What's your birthstone?"

Still, she stared like her life was
flashing before her eyes. "You hit me, Nick."

I kissed her. She drew away, and
I pulled her back. "Your birthday's in
February, right? I'll ask the jeweler what
the stone is."

I held her close until she stopped
struggling. The sun was down, but it wasn't
dark enough for a moon, and we crossed bridges
connecting the islands, Big Pine Key, Plantation
Key, Key Largo. Then we drove through mainland
Miami a while. When we reached home, the sky
above Rickenbacker Causeway was black, and
Caitlin slept on my shoulder.

MARCH 30

8:00 A.M.—Miss Higgins's classroom

> I want to be Ludwig when I grow up.
> I admire Beethoven's musical flair;
> And won't mind when children sneer in disgust;
> At my pickled expression, gorgon hair.

The opening quatrain of a sonnet by Derek Wayne. Higgins slumps in her wheelchair. Me, I'm freaking. I heard nothing about reading these poems aloud. No way can I read this. No way. Derek winds to a close (wish he'd written something longer), and Elsa volunteers.

"Mine's a haiku, Miss Higgins," Elsa says in her most self-important voice. "It's called 'Unseen Violence.'" She reads,

> The dragon's lurking,
> Hidden behind eyes of green
> At a desk so near.

My blood jumps like a fumbled ball. People have been leaving me alone lately, but by syllable twelve of Elsa's poem, every eye meets mine. God, I hate her. I glance sideways, let my eyes sear into hers. She smirks. I remind myself to breathe. Higgins looks from Elsa to me, then back.

"See me after class, Elsa." She turns to me. "We may as well have yours, Nicholas."

"Call on someone else."

"I'm calling on you."

"I can't read mine."

Snickers. Higgins's horseshoe-shaped eyebrows rise still higher. Shock treatment. "You didn't do the assignment?"

"Dog ate his homework," Elsa whispers.

I look at Higgins. "I did it. I just can't read it here." Elsa's stuffing knuckles into her oversized mouth. "It's . . . personal."

"All creative writing is personal, Nicholas."

"My poem's not about Beethoven or dragons." I manage a sneer at Elsa. "I didn't hear you say we had to read it."

Higgins tents her fingers, sizing me up, and for a second, I think she'll cut me a break. No such luck. "If you didn't complete the assignment, I'm afraid I'll have to—"

"Give me an F?" I say. "Fine."

My forehead is tight. I do not want an F. An F is irreparable. With an F, my final grade will be a

B, something I've never gotten in English. And my father will freak.

But that's in the future. Right now, there's only slow death by humiliation if I read.

After class, I wait. I consider begging Higgins to let me write something else, but Elsa's at her desk. Words like *self-control, appropriate, propriety* slither from Higgins's lips, and Elsa nods, saying she had no idea we'd be reading aloud. Still, when she faces me, she's smiling.

"Was your poem about Caitlin?" she whispers, passing my desk.

"No. About you. I couldn't read it because it was pornographic, all my wet dreams about your nonexistent tits and bony elbows."

"Pig." Elsa pulls her books to her chest. "By the way, Caitlin's hot and heavy with some football player."

"Thanks. I knew that."

But hearing it makes me long to do something, long to tell or show or make Caitlin know I'm the one for her. I wait for Elsa to leave, then start for the door.

"Nicholas?"

I turn to face Miss Higgins.

"Didn't you do the assignment?" she asks.

I try to smile. "Don't I always?" I pull the paper from my notebook.

Her whitish eyes take me in. "Yes. You're a good student. I hate to ruin a perfect transcript, but I believe reading aloud is essential to writing. Following instructions is up there too. Why wouldn't you read?"

"I'll write something else and read it tomorrow."

"You must have expected me to see it."

I hold the paper out with my good-student smile. "You can see it." I drop it onto her desk and walk out.

When I enter the hall, a fist rams my face.

"Leave her alone!"

"Caitlin's gone, Nick."

Mrs. McCourt's lacy red negligee left little to the imagination, and her feather-slippered feet sported crimson toenails. I wondered whether she put on fresh polish for bed. I was so busy gaping I barely heard her. I think I managed, "Huh?"

"Caitlin left. I thought she was with you." Mrs. McCourt threw open the door, waving her hand in what was probably meant as an inviting gesture. She offered me a muffin.

But I was out of there before you could say magic crystal. Why did Caitlin leave? I always drove her to school. I jumped into the car, not opening the door. A block later, I saw Caitlin, looking lonely in white pants and a green linen shirt. I pulled beside her.

She turned. Her face looked different, almost out of line. Then, I realized it was her makeup. Heavier than usual, it still didn't cover the red mark under her eye. My breath quickened. I'd done that. How? I'd barely touched her. Her eyes met mine.

She said, "I can't see you anymore, Nick."

I followed, cruising at idle speed. "Why?"

She kept walking. "Why? Because you hit me, Nick. You hit me! You practically kill us driving home in the wrong lane, then you hit me. Does any of this ring a bell?"

She crossed the sidewalk and started walking in people's yards. I ditched the car to run after her. In a few steps, I lost my breath. Impossible. I ran miles at football practice. But Caitlin's words knocked the wind out of me. God, it was a slap, barely a mark. Yet, I was helpless to the point of desperation. I put my hands on her

204

shoulders, and she recoiled like I'd hit her again.

I begged her to give me another chance, but she said, "No. I can't take it. I can't be with someone who hurts me."

She broke into a run, and I chased her like an asshole. I was an asshole. We were near school. The traffic jam had started. Heads whirled at the awesome sight of Nick Andreas chasing the homecoming princess down the street. I barely noticed. I was too busy begging for another chance, telling her what a scum I was, it was all my fault. I was as close to bawling as I get. Bawling about what a loser I was and how I'd do anything to make it up to her. Anything.

She stopped at the parking lot entrance, and cars worked around her. "I'm sorry, Nick."

"But you said you loved me. Is that something you turn on and off?"

"I just can't be with you."

"If you love me, I can change."

Caitlin said she wished she could believe that. Then she turned and started toward the oak tree where our group met every morning. She said she wouldn't tell anyone what happened.

Why was she doing this? I wanted to run, throw myself at her feet. Or maybe grab her shoulders and shake her until she begged me to stop. But she stood by Saint, their bodies perfect as puzzle pieces. I was the one who didn't fit. I trudged to my car. One thing was sure, I'd do anything to get her back.

MARCH 30

My bedroom

The mirror reveals the only black eye I've gotten from anyone but my father. This one's courtesy of Saint. And Tom. Tom was with him.

They'd ambushed me coming from English class. After the punch, Saint grabbed my arms and held them behind my back.

"Leave her alone!" Saint yelled.

I didn't struggle, just looked at him. "What do you mean?" I said, my father's face taking over, his cool eyes appraising Saint's fiery ones. I'd seen that face enough to be able to put it on and off. I hated myself for it.

"You know damn well. Stop calling her! Stop talking to her in the halls! Stop leaving little presents in her locker!" He shook me with every sentence. "She's not interested, okay?"

"Who's not?" I said, cool as he was hot. "Caitlin? I'm not allowed to talk to Caitlin."

"Don't screw with me. We both know you do, and I don't need a court order to kick your ass!" He shoved me against a locker. "Consider this a preview."

"Come on, Nick," Tom pleaded with me. "Just lay off."

I glared at him. "You're not speaking to me, so shut up." I pulled from Saint's grip. "And you're just pissed I got there first."

As I walked away, Saint yelled, "By the way, thanks for the roses. I told her I bought them."

Now, I pull the photograph of Tom and me off the mirror. I look at it a second before I rip it unrecognizable.

I'd been camped on Caitlin's doorstep since two, after a morning spent on the beach, texting her over and over to forgive me. She didn't answer, and there was nowhere else I could think of to be. At five forty-five, Caitlin showed up with Elsa. I demanded to know where she'd been.

"What business is that of yours?" Elsa said. Caitlin fished for her keys, avoiding my eyes.

"We need to talk," I said.

Elsa grabbed Caitlin's arm. "She isn't speaking to you."

"Aren't you supposed to be somewhere?" I said. When Elsa didn't move, I thrust a silver-wrapped package toward Caitlin.

"I can't, Nick."

It's hard for me to admit this, even to a notebook. Even to myself. But at that point, I begged. Flat-out begged her to open it. It was my only chance. I sank to my knees, not caring how I looked. Nothing mattered. Nothing.

And finally, Caitlin gave in. She pulled from Elsa's grip, eyes weary under her heavy makeup. I straightened. She took the package, peeled off the paper, gasping at the leather-crested box. She opened it.

The amethyst caught the sun's dying rays from its diamond perch. Caitlin's eyes widened.

"I was going to wait 'til Christmas," I said. "But there won't be Christmas without you. There's nothing good for me without you." Elsa made the "tiny violin" gesture with thumb and forefinger, but Caitlin turned the box in her hand. "Put it on," I said.

Elsa's voice. "She won't take you back just because—"

"I love you, Caitlin." I ignored Elsa.

"Caitlin, you can't be bought with some trinket." Elsa was angry. She pointed to

Caitlin. "You think I haven't noticed that big, red mark on your face? He did that to you."

"No, I didn't."

"Did he?" Elsa demanded. "Caitlin?"

Caitlin was silent. We stood there a long time. Caitlin looked from me to Elsa, then back. Finally, she said, "Of course not."

"Oh, God! You're such a liar! You should be happy together, a liar and a criminal." Elsa stormed into the street, not checking for traffic.

Caitlin started to follow. I stopped her, saying, "Try it on, Cat."

"I don't know."

"You're going to let her boss you around?" I slipped the box from Caitlin's hand and removed the ring. I took her hand. When she didn't pull away, I eased the ring over her knuckle. "Give me a chance, Cat."

"I don't know."

"So, you don't love me anymore?"

Caitlin didn't answer. Mrs. McCourt's car pulled into the garage. I heard footsteps in the house. Then she was in our faces. She winked at me, barely looking at Caitlin.

"Your hair's a mess. Can't believe he stays around with you looking like that." She smiled at me again. I still held Caitlin's hand and saw Mrs. McCourt's eyes go from my face to our hands. They lit on the ring. "Where'd you get that?"

Caitlin raised her head. "Nick gave it to me."

"Give it back. A young lady does not accept jewelry from a gentleman." She turned her shadowed eyes on me. "Where does a boy your age get that kind of money?"

Caitlin muttered something about dealing cocaine, and her mother said, "Sarcasm isn't attractive."

"Who's being sarcastic?" Caitlin said.

Mrs. McCourt shook her head. "Caitlin can't keep the ring, Nick."

"I'm keeping it," Caitlin said, which was news to me. She crossed her arms, stuffing the ringed hand between elbow and breast. "I'd think you'd be happy someone buys me a present, but no. You're jealous."

"Don't be ridiculous."

Caitlin didn't respond. Mrs. McCourt

yanked her into the house and slammed the door. I walked to the driveway, unsure whether I was high as a concert audience or lower than a flea at an NBA convention.

When I got to the car, I heard my name. I searched the pink shutters for an open window. I walked toward it. I could barely see through the screen, but she held up her hand, and the ring gleamed.

"I'll keep it," she said.

"To piss off your mother?"

"She sent me to my room—can you believe it?" Caitlin rattled the screen until it detached. She stuck her hand under and reached for mine. "It's not the ring, it's you. All day, I've thought about what you said about changing. How you loved me. I didn't tell anyone we broke up except Elsa. Big mistake."

"Was it?"

She nodded. The black screen didn't dull her blue eyes when she said, "I love you, Nick. I want to be with you. I just want you not to hit me."

I promised I wouldn't, and she said, "I believe you."

MARCH 30

9:00 P.M.—Mustard Watermelon Bar, South Miami

"Hello?"

The pay phone smells of booze and hairspray. I grip it, taking a swig of beer. Across the room, Leo, in someone's University of Miami baseball jersey, tries his moves on a redhead. Caitlin's voice fills my ear.

"Why are you doing this, Nick?"

She's different. At least, she sounds different to me. *Wheel of Fortune* blares in the background, and Caitlin sounds used up. Is it Saint's threats? Mario's nagging?

No, it's me. The only thing that's changed is me.

"Please leave me alone," Caitlin's new voice says, and I want to obey if it would make her sound happier. Leo gestures from the bar. I wave him off, closing my eyes, trying for the feeling I used to get with Caitlin, how it felt to know she loved me. Could love me. No good.

"Please, Nick."

Leo calls my name when Cat says it. I push the receiver button, leave the half-full beer on the ledge, and find Leo. He's added a blond to his circle, over-ripe but borderline beautiful and obviously meant for me. She smiles. Leo palms my shoulder.

"Nick, meet Laura." He sees her notice my black eye. "Nick got hit with a baseball."

Cut the crap. But I nod and straddle the barstool. Laura leans against me, smelling like the telephone did, and I feel the roundness of her breast on my arm. I don't react.

"Can I get you something?" the bartender asks.

"You have Mountain Dew?" I ask, suddenly remembering Mario's rule about no alcohol. Why am I even here?

The bartender shakes his head. "This isn't McDonald's."

"Order a beer," Laura says. But I wave the guy off and look at Leo. He's making out with the redhead. I wonder where Neysa is tonight. Laura watches me, putting her hand on my butt. I don't react. Finally, she says, "What are you, gay?"

"That's it." I leave her standing there and return to the telephone. I fumble for Mario's card. He said call him anytime. I stare at his name a minute before shoving the card back into my wallet. I call a cab.

I fall, painfully sober, into bed. When I wake, the digital clock flashes 12:00. My watch says 8:30. I'm late for school. I remember I'd been dreaming of Caitlin, and I roll over, longing to dream of her one last time.

214

Later, when I wake up for the second time

The first thing I do is pick up the journal. Funny, I didn't want to write in it. Now, I'm way over the word count I needed. I could probably stop. But I have to see this through to the end. If I don't, I have the feeling I'll drown.

So, I was being careful again, freaking about whether I'd make a wrong move. Sometimes, I heard Elsa's voice, _He did that to you,_ and saw Caitlin running from me. But Caitlin wore my ring, and everyone knew she was my girl.

At school, Tom was big news. Back in October, he'd bet Liana that if an opposing team scored ten points on our defense, he'd get a short haircut. Liana had been lobbying for that anyway. "What if you win?" I'd asked once. "If no one scores ten points? You get anything good?"

He smiled. "Not like you mean, little buddy. Liana said she'd cook me dinner."

I'd called him a sucker. But by late November, no one had scored ten against us, and Tom got the credit. Key was having its first winning season, and if we won the last game, scheduled to coincide with Key's annual Winterfest carnival, we'd make the regionals.

"What she doesn't know is, if I lose, I'm shaving my head," Tom said as we walked to the chorus room to meet Caitlin one day after returning from Key West. Two guys, hands still greasy from auto shop, accosted Tom, wanting to rub his head for luck. One guy even called Tom Samson. I said I guessed that made Liana Delilah.

Tom didn't answer because at that second, Caitlin rushed from the chorus room, Derek Wayne hot on her heels. Derek was saying, "You know you want to do it," and Caitlin giggled, practically crashing into us.

"Do what?" I asked, giving Derek my best glare.

"Oh, nothing." Caitlin tried to pull me toward the parking lot. Derek walked away.

I didn't budge. "I want to know what Wayne the Brain wants you to do."

"It's silly. Just, Mrs. Reyes said I should try out for the Winterfest talent show."

"That's great, Cat," Tom said. "If she

asked you, she must think you're really good—like when Coach told me to bulk up so I could be starting linebacker. He couldn't say that if the position wasn't available."

I was getting a little sick of Tom and football. Caitlin was beaming, and I said, "Wouldn't that take a lot of time, though? You've got your sorority meetings."

We were approaching the parking lot, and suddenly it was like a conga line heading for Tom—except the music was more Insane Clown Posse than Gloria Estefan. Several generic-looking cheerleader types approached Tom about being a target in Friday's pie-throwing raffle. Liana materialized from the crowd, along with a reporter from Keynotes. Dave "Doobie" Dooley, who smoked pot behind the bushes mornings before school, threw himself at Tom's shoulders, shrieking, "Don't let her scalp you, man!" Some freshman JV players followed, giving Tom we're not worthy gestures. I steered Caitlin around the carnage. Once we broke from Tom, we walked alone.

We reached the car, and I opened Caitlin's door. "I don't want you in that talent show." I didn't like it. She'd have extra practices. Then be parading herself on stage for everyone to see.

"But Tom said . . ."

"The gridiron hero's a music critic now?"

"He had a point."

"So, go out with Tom." When Caitlin started to protest, I said, "Look, I'm trying to protect you. I've heard you sing. You suck. I don't want you embarrassing both of us."

She started babbling about what Mrs. Reyes had said, and I said, "Are you deaf or just stupid? I said no. Subject closed." Why did she have to do stuff to set me off? I saw my fist clench in my lap.

Caitlin saw it too. She stared at my hand, then at my face. Finally, she said, "I guess you're right. I'm really not good enough."

"That's my girl." I put my arm around her, kissing her. "Will your mom be late tonight?"

"Probably around seven."

"So I'll come over after practice."

"Sure," she said, and I kissed her again.

Tom and Liana finally broke from the crowd, and we drove to Mr. Pizza together. Caitlin didn't mention the talent show again, and neither did Tom. Still, it nagged at me. All I'd had to do was make a fist, and she'd given in. Or _had_ she?

APRIL 1

Passing period after Miss Higgins's English class

"Where did you get the black eye?" Higgins asks after class Wednesday, pointing two red-tipped index fingers at my face. Behind me, second period drifts to their desks.

"Present from an old friend."

"Same friend as last time?"

"Last time?" I feel suddenly warm despite the air-conditioned cool.

"January, I believe," she says.

I don't flinch. "No. Then, I was training for boxing. Had to give it up, though. Interfered with my poetry."

Higgins pulls her grade book from the top drawer and flips through its pages. She doesn't smile. "You missed two days in October, came back with bruises."

"Flu."

"A day in January—fat lip."

"Cold sore."

"Now this."

"This wasn't—"

"Mrs. Walters noticed the same pattern last year."

"It's not what you think," I say.

"What do I think?" Higgins draws breath between slightly parted teeth. I can't avoid her eyes. She knows about my father. From my poem, maybe, and my face. But what does that mean? Teachers are supposed to report child abuse, but I'm not a child. I'm sixteen, old enough to take care of myself. I shift my suddenly immense weight from foot to foot.

Breathe.

I give her a Nick Andreas smile, meeting her eyes with my good one. "That I have lots of enemies?"

"Or one enemy," she says. "Someone at home, perhaps?"

I gesture at my eye. "My dad didn't do this."

"I don't believe you."

I shrug and walk away, almost breaking into a run at the door. I don't think I breathe until I get to chemistry class, but my mind is racing. If Higgins says anything to my father, he'll just get meaner.

The sound of ice cubes greeted me. In my father's house, ice cubes are air-raid sirens that send me diving for cover. I searched for an exit. There was none. Usually, I missed happy hour, my father's version of dinner at home, but he was early, I was late, and worlds collided. My father swirled his glass. I tried to look casual—impossible—and walked past him.

"Hi, Dad."

He gestured me closer. The clink of ice against crystal intensified, and I began the countdown in my head . . . ten, nine, eight . . . I walked toward him . . . three, two . . . He brandished a wrapped condom between two fingers like a witness with the bloody glove. "This is yours?"

Nailed. As in crucified, in the true, biblical sense of the word. I hung back, trying to avoid the inevitable blow. I stared at the evidence.

"Answer me."

I stepped toward the stairway. He didn't react, and I glanced back at him, expecting the worst, bracing myself. Finally, I said, "Yes, sir."

My father smiled. He sat in his antique wing chair against the backdrop of Biscayne Bay, clutching his crystal glass and grinning like I'd never seen. "Congratulations."

I figured I must have heard him wrong. I said, "What?"

"Congratulations, my son, for becoming a man."

I felt marble beneath my feet. My

fingers relaxed. My father was proud. Of me. For years, I'd brought home perfect report cards, trying to make him happy. But now, he was proud. Is this the only thing that makes me a man in your eyes? I wanted to scream it. But that clinking ice brought reality back. My father was finally proud of me.

I smiled. "Thank you, sir."

He gestured toward the leather sofa beside him. He poured another scotch, filling his glass almost to overflowing, drank half and filled it again. He filled a second glass halfway and thrust it toward me. He raised his drink. "To my son becoming a man."

I drank with him. I'd had scotch before, but this tasted different, bitter. Impossible. My father bought the best. He asked me if I had a girlfriend. I took another sip—still bitter—and nodded. "Her name's Caitlin."

This he ignored, reaching for his wallet. He pulled out a wad of bills, hundreds, who knows how many, and leaned forward, fanning them in front of him. "Buy her something nice. Then, give her a hundred, and tell her

to get some pills because these things . . ."
With the money, he gestured toward the
condom, thrown on the glass table. "These
things do not work." He shoved the bills
at me and refilled his glass. I heard the
waves, the pale liquid sloshing against
crystal, and his question. "Do you know how
I know this, Nicos?"

I nodded. I'd heard it before, too many
times to care. I met his eyes, not taking
the money. His smile was gone. He dropped
the bills onto the table. I threw back the
rest of my scotch.

"Sixteen years old," he said. "I came to
this country with nothing. I worked, joined
the navy, went to school. I made an error."
He stopped and refilled my glass before
emptying his own. "For one mistake, I was
to pay, to marry a nothing whose family
barely kept her in shoes. I paid once. I
will not pay again." He slammed the empty
bottle to the glass table. "You must not
make my mistake, Nicos."

I nodded. I was the mistake. But I
was numb to it. I felt the scotch's heat
inside my body, in my toes, my fingertips.

I didn't drink any more. I also didn't point out the obvious, that he was rich anyway. My father was silent, his green eyes expecting no answer, and finally, I stood, took the money, said, "I'll do that, Dad," and shoved the wad into my pocket. I counted to three before I added, "Okay if I go study at Tom's now?"

He nodded, and I walked back to the door. His voice stopped me.

"Nicos?" I turned, hand on the knob. He was smiling again, eyes half-closed, slumped in his chair. "You were a tough little bastard, Nicos, tough like me. You wanted to be born."

I nodded. The glass slipped from his hand and shattered against the marble floor. I was out of there. I sprinted down the driveway, not knowing where I was going, and jumped into my car. I roared into the night, wanting to scatter my father's money, like his words, to the December wind.

APRIL 2

Miss Higgins's classroom

Thursday morning, there's an envelope on my desk addressed to my father. My vital organs dance a jig as I turn it over. Not sealed. Casting a glance around the room, I slip the sharp paper from its ice-blue envelope.

The stationery is the blue FROM THE DESK OF type. The handwriting, elderly. I read:

Dear Mr. Andreas,

It has been my experience that children reflect the lessons learned at home. Therefore, you are to be congratulated on your fine son.

Nicholas is an exemplary student in my class and a valued member of the Key Biscayne High community. He is intelligent, innovative, and reliable. I am certain the affection and understanding he receives from you play a part in that.

Please give your son the respect he deserves.
Sincerely, Laetitia Higgins

I stand there, chuckling at first at her characterization of my father's "affection and understanding." On second reading, the phrases attack me, too saccharine

226

and pointed to misinterpret. I realize Higgins and I have an agreement. She knows. She wants my father to know she knows, but she won't get me in trouble. Why does she even care? After class, I read it again, leaning against the white-tiled men's room wall. How much of what she said about me is true?

At noon, I go to her. She crams her paperback under her cafeteria box lunch when I enter, but not before I notice the title, *Love's Savage Fury*. She grimaces.

"You were expecting, maybe, *The Iliad*?" she says.

I smile, hesitating in the center of the room with nowhere to put my hands. Finally, I approach her desk and lean against it. "You wrote to my father."

"You read it, then?"

"No, I—"

"I meant for you to read it."

"Then I read it," I say, smiling. "Thank you."

"No thanks are necessary. What I wrote about *you* was truthful."

I look at her gnarled hands playing on her calendar blotter. "You know about—"

"Your trouble with the law?" she says, rescuing me before I say anything about my father, anything that might require her to do or say something I don't want done or said. I nod.

"Yes, I know." She reaches into her drawer and pulls

out a stack of papers, the poetry assignment. "Doing something wrong, even something hurtful, doesn't mean you're a bad person, Nicholas, not at sixteen."

"I know that."

"Do you? I wasn't certain." Her watery blue eyes meet mine a second, and she smiles. She whisks a sheet from the stack of papers. My poem. It's not graded, but she's written "See me" across the top, "See me" being teacherese for "Call the guys in the white coats."

"See you?"

"I advise the school's literary journal, the *Seagull*. I thought the writer might wish to submit some other work. When I saw it was you, I knew you wouldn't."

"Why's that?"

"Wouldn't suit your image."

"Didn't know I had one." But I can't help it. I give her a Nick Andreas smile.

She looks away. "Your image precedes you into the room. You should try leaving it home sometime."

The warning bell rings and I hear the hallway sounds. "Look," I say. "I just wanted to thank you." She nods, and I shove the paper into my notebook. I collect my backpack and start to leave. I turn back. "Was my poem really any good?"

She nods again, chewing a bite of cafeteria hoagie

before saying, "Think about what I said."

I keep walking, but I'm picturing myself, dressed in black, reading poetry in a dimly lit coffeehouse.

My room, later that day

I can't help taking out the poem again. I feel kind of weird about it. It takes me a minute to realize the weird feeling is pride. Maybe I can actually write. What a laugh. It's just a stupid poem. But no one's ever really said I was good at anything before. I reread it. The content strikes me again. I miss Tom—even though he doesn't deserve it.

After drinking with my father, I thought I'd end up at Caitlin's. But when my motor stopped, I was in Tom's driveway. It was eleven-thirty. I'd driven two hours to travel two blocks. I grabbed the packed gym bag I always kept in my trunk and walked to the patio door. Tom let me in, unquestioning. Still, I told him my father had a woman over. If Tom knew I was lying, he never mentioned it. I followed him down the hall.

The great thing about Tom's room was it never changed. It evolved, maybe, over the years, with Pokemon posters replaced by

Miley Cyrus, then Taylor Swift. But if you looked on his top closet shelf, next to the Barron's SAT Prep, there'd still be bags of plastic army men and enough Tonka trucks for a major construction project. He'd deny it, but they were there. Tom sat, texting. I saw him type nick here.

Liana's reply appeared. Hi, Nick.

I took Tom's phone and typed Hi. Then I flopped onto the bottom bunk of the bunk bed Tom had begged for when we were eight. I buried my face in the old University of Florida bedspread. I loved the smell of the sheets at Tom's house. I knew it was just bleach, but to me, it was home. I took out my Spanish workbook and spent the next half hour making pointless marks in it. Tom's two-fingered typing punctuated the silence. I finished the assignment, then walked to his chair and stood over him. He turned to me. "You mind?"

I looked away, let him have his tender moment. Finally, he put the phone down, and I said, "You at least sexting?"

"What do you think? Liana's mom turns off her phone at 9."

"I think Liana's mother's been watching too many talk shows."

I walked into the bathroom. I even kept a toothbrush there. I used it and got into bed. The desk lamp was off, so the only light was the glow from the Dilbert screensaver. Tom hoisted himself to the top bunk. The bed always creaked when he did that. Was my father still in the living room, drinking? Could Tom's father ever do that? Impossible. Springs sagged above me, and suddenly I wanted to talk, wanted to tell Tom everything, things I'd never told him or anyone. Not only about my father but about me and Cat, that sometimes I felt so out of control with her. But about my father too, how afraid I was of becoming like him. Tom shifted in bed. I asked him if he was awake.

When he said yes, I said, "Do you and your dad ever fight? I mean, argue about anything?"

"Sure, doesn't everyone?"

"Like, what?"

"Stupid stuff, mostly. Grades, helping around the house. His ongoing thing's my hair, same as Liana's. You know he offered to buy me a boat if I cut it short?"

"Sailboat or powerboat?"

"Doesn't matter. If I take it, it'll never end. I mean, you think my hair's stupid, but you accept it. You accept _me_. My parents just want me to be like everyone else. Last week, my mom said, 'Nick always looks so neat.'" He laughed. "This stupid bet's the worst thing. If we win the Winterfest game, we go to the regionals, but I don't care. I'm just worried about not having to cut my hair."

I heard quick, light footsteps. The door opened, and something landed on my bed. "Wimpy's here."

"Yeah, dumb dog loves you." Tom's head disappeared from view, and I thought he'd gone to sleep until he said, "How about you and your dad?"

I stroked Wimpy's bumpy fur. Then I let my hand drop to the side of the bed. I couldn't tell Tom. His problems were normal, the kind on Very Special Episodes of TV sitcoms. Mine were intense foreign films. What could I say: <u>By the way, my father</u>

calls me a mistake, and I slapped Caitlin on the way back from Key West? What could Tom do besides think I was subhuman? Maybe he'd even be right. Finally, I said, "You know. He's not around much, doesn't care what I do. Guess he likes work better." Wimpy warmed my feet.

"You're lucky," Tom said.

"Maybe so."

I lay there, listening to Tom's breathing become even with sleep, the stop and start of the central air. The last time I looked, the digital clock said two-thirty. I always wondered if things would have turned out different if I'd talked to Tom that night.

APRIL 4

Mario's class

"How did you feel then?"

Somehow, I'm telling Mario and the world about the fight Caitlin and I had on the Seven Mile Bridge. Mario ambles toward me, plants his feet, and says, "What emotion were you feeling then?"

"What emotion?"

"Name it, it's yours."

"Guess I was pissed off."

Mario sighs audibly. "Are you ever anything else?"

Why is he yanking my chain? I don't have to listen. I push the *off* button.

I sit.

"Well?" he says.

"Thought it was rhetorical."

"You thought wrong." Mario places a hairy hand on my shoulder. "What, my volatile boy, did you feel besides *pissed off*?"

I don't feel like answering.

"Here are some choices." Mario smiles, patient, a botanist waiting for flowers to grow. "Were you afraid? Embarrassed? Ashamed of being a jerk to the woman you supposedly loved?"

"You said no put-downs." I stand, my shoulder brushing his gut.

"Am I embarrassing you?" Still angelic.

"No." I look into ten eyes. Are they laughing? "What's your point?"

"You've got two speeds, pissed off and asleep. You can't operate like that. You've got to acknowledge other emotions, other ways of dealing with them." He starts to walk away, then turns. "Your girlfriend says something you think questions your manhood, so you call her a bitch. Or a whore. Or whatever particular term of endearment you learned at your father's knee. Next time, you figure she asked for it, so you hit her. Is that the best thing to do?"

"I don't know."

"Do you want to know? Think!"

Outside, a guy and girl jog by. I watch them slow to a walk, first her, then him. He swings an arm to grab her, and she stops, leans toward him. They kiss. Then again, his free hand caressing her hair.

"I don't know," I repeat. But the words are hollow.

"That's great," Mario says. "No, really. It's great you're proud of what you did." He leans over me. "Whoooee! Nick Andreas is a hero! He can lick any girl he wants!"

"Screw you." Behind my eyes feels suddenly hot.

"I'm pissing you off?" Mario says.

"Yes."

He leans closer, on me like tight briefs. No one else moves. He waves a chubby forefinger in my eyes. "So you're pissed."

"Yes." Swallowing.

"You're madder than my fat brother, Julio, when someone beats him to the dinner table?"

"Yes."

Across from me, A.J.'s mouth hangs open.

"Then hit me," Mario whispers.

"What?"

"Did I stutter? Hit me." When I don't budge, Mario yells in my face, "Hit me!"

Instead, I elbow past him, the running girl's image still tattooed on my brain. "I can't."

Mario follows. "Why the hell not? You chicken?"

"Quit it."

"No. You're mad, aren't you?"

"Right."

"When you got mad at Caitlin, you hit her?"

"I slapped her." But it's no different, even to me.

"Hit her, slapped her. You didn't turn the other cheek, adopt this Gandhi posture you're taking here, did you?" When I shake my head, he says, "So you're mad at me, you hit me. Right?"

"You're a teacher."

"It's okay to hit your girlfriend, but not a teacher?"

"I didn't say that," I say.

"You didn't have to. You say it with every molecule of your being."

I look away. "I know it's not okay."

"But you can't control yourself?" I shake my head, just to get rid of him, and sit down again. The room's so quiet I swear I hear my hair blowing in the air conditioner. Mario nudges Tiny over and sits by me.

"Sure you can," he says. "You just did it with me. You can do the same with her."

I should have hit him when I had the chance.

The rest of class, Mario lectures about the three C's, compromise, communication, and control. Near the end, Kelly says, "Hey, Mario, what do you call a woman with two black eyes?"

"We're not doing that today," Mario says.

Kelly stops, but when Mario turns away, Kelly whispers, "The new and improved model."

After class, I gather my stuff, hanging back so I'm the last to go. When everyone's gone, I approach Mario. The fluorescent lights buzz overhead.

"That day on the bridge, when I slapped Caitlin . . ."

"Yeah?" He turns to give me his full attention.

"I was afraid, okay? I was afraid she'd leave me."

Mario nods. "I know you were." He starts to reach his hand out, then takes it back when he sees my face. "It's okay to be afraid, Nick."

I shrug and walk out. Tiny's waiting outside. He offers me a ride home. I'd take him up on it, but today I'm meeting Leo. We're banging out some school-required community service hours by selling sodas at a carnival. Our shift begins at noon.

At five after, I'm still waiting. I remember when we discussed lateness in class. I'm annoyed with Leo but not furious. Would I be madder at Cat? Losing it, maybe? No. Not really.

Maybe.

Probably.

No time to consider. Leo's black Trans Am cruises to a stop. When I get in, he says, "Sorry we're late. *Someone* got held up at the drugstore." He turns to the guilty party, Neysa, sitting beside him. "That's your story, right?"

"Leo . . ." she says.

"Leo . . ." he imitates, gunning the motor.

"Why are you acting this way in front of—"

"What way?" Leo demands over the tires' squeal. "*You're* the problem, not me."

"I'm sorry." Neysa examines the floor mat.

"I'm sorry," Leo mocks. "I'm sorry I'm always late. I'm sorry I'm a lying slut. I'm sorry I—"

"It's okay," I tell Neysa. "I don't think it matters if we're late." Leo, I ignore. Why is he acting like this? Why is it so familiar?

The Grove traffic is heavy, and Leo swerves, barely avoiding cars to the front and side, eyeing Neysa, not the road. "I don't appreciate being lied to," he says. "Or waiting, with your parents giving me the evil eye while you're out catting around." Leo floors it through a yellow light, and Neysa clutches the door handle. "Am I scaring you, princess?"

"Quit it," I tell him.

He glances back like he forgot I was there. "Quit what?"

I look at Neysa. Her eyes plead with me to say nothing. "Quit driving like a maniac," I say.

Leo slows, saying nothing.

We reach the fairgrounds twenty minutes late. The sun scorches, melting wads of cotton candy and blobs of ice cream dropped on the ground. The air is filled with the odor of hot dogs and burnt sugar, a smell that, like everything else, reminds me of Caitlin. We were at Winterfest carnival the day she left me for good. Leo, Neysa, and I find our booth in silence, a trailer manned by two girls from Palmetto High. Neysa and I get to work. Leo does nothing, just palms the counter, watching Neysa. When a customer is male, she steps back, letting me or one of the Palmetto girls help him. I want to ask why. Why is Leo acting like a poster boy for female chastity? But Neysa's eyes stop me. She's afraid of him. No wonder. If he acts like this around people, what's he like when they're alone?

The afternoon is slow and I'm slower. Around two-thirty, three guys ask for Neysa. She goes to help them, then stops. Steps back. Leo shoves past.

"Just get the ice," he says.

"Hello to you too, Leo," the biggest guy, a rich kid trying to look like a gangsta, says as Neysa obeys Leo's command.

If looks could kill, the guy would be two hundred pounds of medical waste.

"Hello, Alejandro," Leo says. "Visiting my girlfriend?"

"Could be." Alejandro smiles. "Don't sell yourself short. Maybe I'm visiting you."

"That's a given. You visit Neysa, you visit me."

Leo brushes melted ice from the counter and yells to Neysa, "You got that ice yet?"

"Yes." Neysa hands Leo three cups, not looking up.

"Yes, *sir*," Alejandro corrects. "Give my man Leo the respect he deserves."

Neysa's lip twitches. "*Por favor*, Alex," she whispers. "Please don't start with him."

Behind us, the roller coaster's in gear. Boys laugh. Girls scream, but I don't listen. A family passes, the daughter hanging from her father's shoulders. Twin boys in matching Scooby-Doo T-shirts sprint for the shooting gallery. I don't watch. I hear Leo's voice. I see Leo's eyes. I don't like what I see.

"Why don't we go," I say, and the Palmetto girls volunteer to cover for us.

"Because Neysa isn't through serving her friends." Leo pulls Neysa to the counter. Ice flies everywhere. "Now, clean it up!" He raises his hand, and she backs away.

"*Leoncito*, not here." Neysa's eyes are huge in her face.

Leo releases her, suddenly calm. "Neysa, your manners. Ask Alex what else he wants."

Neysa doesn't move.

"Do it!"

Neysa shakes her head at Alejandro. "What else would you like?"

"To give you a ride home," Alejandro says, and Leo's shoulders constrict.

"I have a ride home." Neysa indicates Leo.

I go to help a family. Through their chatter, I hear Alejandro say, "You stay long enough, he'll kill you."

But Neysa pats Leo's hand. "We understand each other."

Alejandro shrugs and signals to his friends. They walk away toward the rides, whirling and sick-inducing. Across the midway, a monster in a cape scares passersby, inviting them into his haunted mansion. Three little girls in cornrows hug one another in fright. But I see Leo's black eyes.

Later, when Leo drops me off, I watch his taillights to the end of the block, then beyond until they're like distant stars. I don't plan to see him again.

Ten minutes later, in my room

God, was I like that with Caitlin?

Saint was shirtless, and I was sick about it. A few days before Winterfest, the school's annual football game and carnival, we had lunch at the beach. Saint was still trying to lose Tom's suntan tattoo. He'd offered a reward for the culprit's name, but I never told. Maybe if he'd noticed the dolphin, still branded on Tom's leg, he'd have figured it out. I was eating Kentucky Fried Chicken strips, trying not to look at Saint, who was letting Peyton spread suntan lotion on his back. Caitlin and I hadn't argued in close to two weeks. Her amethyst ring glittered in the sun as she ate her usual raw carrots.

"Does it ever occur to you that no one wants to see your armpit hair when they're eating?" I asked Saint finally, my arm around Caitlin.

"No, it never does," Saint said. Having spread suntan lotion on every part of his back except Tom's lettering, he lay on his stomach and let Peyton feed him chicken. Between bites, he spoke to Caitlin. "Heard you at rehearsal yesterday. You got some voice."

"Rehearsal?" I asked.

"For the talent show." He turned to the rest of the group, saying, "Bunch of guys are doing an act, and Caitlin's got a solo."

"You do?" Liana and I both said at once. Liana started babbling about how wonderful that was. I said nothing, just looked at Cat. She sat only an inch away, but her eyes were elsewhere. Why had she defied me? She knew how I felt, yet she'd gone to an audition and rehearsals without telling me. Didn't I matter to her? I stared until my eyes felt ready to burst. Finally, someone changed the subject, and Caitlin looked at me. She flinched. I mouthed one word, <u>No</u>.

Caitlin looked away, whining something about hoping I'd change my mind. I ignored her. I dropped my hand from her shoulder and turned to Ashley, who was talking to Peyton. I said, "Say, Ash, I just found out Caitlin's in a talent show Saturday night. Want to go?"

Ashley stopped talking and flipped her auburn hair. "Of course I'm going. Everyone is."

"I meant with me," I said. "Seems the seat next to mine's open. Seat in my car too." I leaned close, ignoring Caitlin. If she didn't care what I thought, I'd teach her a lesson.

"You messing with me?" Ashley asked, so I knew she still liked me.

244

"No way," I said. "We'll have dinner after. Rusty Pelican's nice." I cast a sidelong glance at Cat. The Rusty Pelican was our place, where we'd gone for each month's anniversary. The third one was that week. I could see Caitlin's lips pressed together, her eyes ready to spill.

Ashley said, "Sure I'll go."

"Why are you doing this, Nick?" Caitlin asked.

"Doing what? You're the one doing it to me." Everyone pretended to continue their own conversations, but they watched us. I said to Caitlin, "I don't want you embarrassing yourself in that talent show. You go there, singing like you do, looking like a fat slob, and people will laugh." I was so worked up, I almost believed what I said.

Caitlin did believe it. She metamorphosed with my words, arms drooping at her sides. She said, "Okay, I won't sing. It was a stupid idea."

"I'm only saying this for your own good." I twined my arm around her waist, loving the feel of her hair against my lips.

"Someday, you'll realize I want what's best for you."

"So our date's off," Ashley interrupted. "You used me to get Caitlin to change her mind."

I looked from one to the other. "We can all go together."

"Like I want to be your second-choice date, Nick Andreas." But a minute later, she leaned toward me and said in a whisper everyone could hear, "Call me when you guys break up."

Caitlin said nothing, but her grip tightened around my waist.

My room

I *was* like Leo.

APRIL 11

9:30 A.M.—Mario's class

Something's wrong with Mario. He's pacing like a tiger on a treadmill. He hasn't said much of anything this class. For some reason, my mind turns to Leo. I've avoided him since the carnival last week, not wanting to deal with what I now realize is his abusiveness. Who am I to say anything? But I've heard his voice, leaving frantic messages on my answering machine. Neysa left him. He wants back in the group so she'll see he's changed. No, that won't help. He doesn't know what to do.

I don't either. I ignore the messages.

Now, I watch the train roar past the window. Mario still paces. Kelly asks how many Cubans it takes to screw in a lightbulb, and Mario yells, "Can't you ever just shut up?"

"What about anger control, Mario?" Tiny's teeth flash white. "What about your three C's, or do only we have to abide by that?"

Mario stops pacing. "Yeah, Tyrone, I'm supposed to control myself. And I am. I'm not going around hurting people like some animal, am I? Like . . ." He sinks into his chair, looking first at the ceiling, then our faces. He's silent a long time.

"Look," he finally says, real soft. "It's a bad day, but that's no excuse. Everyone read ahead so there's no homework."

The others obey without comment, but I can't read. I don't know why. I watch Mario instead. He's turned away, but I sense if I could see his face, I'd see tears. What's wrong? Probably nothing, a fight with his wife, maybe. But when his receptionist comes in, I hear the word *newspaper*. I hear Leo's name. Mario slips, unlooking, from his seat, and I take out my journal to forget the killing questions. What did Leo do? And why is the newspaper calling Mario?

The day Caitlin and I broke up began typically. Tom was a hero. At Winterfest carnival, everyone was talking about how Tom "Samson" Carter had held Columbus High to seven points and won his bet with Liana. We'd lost 7-3, but Columbus scored the touchdown when Tom-the-hero wasn't even on the field. It was an offensive fumble, recovered by Columbus and run in to score. One guess who fumbled. Good guess. We were out of the regionals, and it was my fault. When Caitlin tried to say it was no big deal, I told her to shut the hell up. And she did.

Saturday morning, we stood in line for the Himalaya, one of those spinning rides that stays on the ground while loud music and g-forces combine to produce thrills, chills, etc. I wasn't thrilled that day. On the ride, people screamed "Faster! Faster!" and the carnies egged them on. I could have waited forever. I'd dragged myself to the carnival because my friends were going, and if I didn't, they'd know I was laying low. My fist clenched around Caitlin's hand. She tensed beside me. Finally, the ride ground to a stop, and everyone stirred in their seats. We were next.

The first people off the ride were Elsa and Derek.

"Nick!" Elsa said with exaggerated congeniality. "I am so glad to see you. I brought you a present." She flipped a bottle of Elmer's Glue-All at me. When I reached up to grab it, she said, "Good catch, Nick. I wish I'd given it to you sooner. It might have helped."

I hurled the bottle back at her and pulled Caitlin onto the ride. I was strapping us into the light blue and white car when

Derek yelled something to Cat. Something about only eight hours to showtime.

The ride lurched to a start, and we began our first circuit around the track. Outside, there were faces, people waiting, friends waving, everyone staring and pointing at the loser who'd ruined the season. Caitlin hugged me. I asked her what Derek had meant.

"I don't know," she said.

I said I thought she did. The ride music invaded my brain until I could barely recognize my thoughts. My head pounded. Caitlin's next words were lost in sound and speed. Her mouth moved, her face contorted with the motion of the ride. She looked ugly. I yelled that I couldn't hear her.

She put her mouth against my ear. "I guess he thinks I'm singing."

"Why would he think that?"

"My name's in the program," Cat yelled.

"Faster! Faster!" the riders screamed. The ride operator screamed back at them to yell louder. The noise deafened. Next to me, Caitlin screamed with the crowd.

I yelled too, but what I yelled was, "You're not singing!"

Caitlin backed away. "I'm not," she mouthed. "I told you I'm not!"

I said she'd better not be. I grabbed her arm and held it. The ride lurched and jumped then wound down to the ground. "You'd better not be," I repeated as we slid to a stop. I pulled her out of her seat almost before she undid her seatbelt. We moved toward the exit. At the gate, Josh Brandon, a skinny, unwashed-looking kid from my chemistry class, knocked against me.

"Hey, Andreas, I ever tell you you're my hero?" He nudged the redhead standing by him. "Really. It takes guts to play that bad."

I shoved him back. "You value your life?"

He slipped through the gate, but his obnoxious voice followed me until we reached the cotton candy stand.

The rest of the day was the same, and maybe I was looking for a fight. I found one.

A MINUTE LATER

Mario's empty classroom

Mario hasn't returned by the end of class. The others leave. I put my pen in my backpack, unable to write further, waiting for Mario. My head feels like rap music's playing inside, and I stare at the ceiling fan. Finally, I hear the doorknob. Mario comes in. "Nick."

I turn. He stares at the floor, pressing his lips together. Finally, he says, "You were friends . . . weren't you, with Leo?"

I nod, remembering our last encounter.

Mario sits by me. His face is weary, his eyes rimmed red.

"It never gets easier," he says. "When I started doing this, they told me, you win some, you lose some. Always think about the ones you're helping, but . . ." His head twitches. "Leo's dead, Nick."

The room is silent except for Mario's voice and the ceiling fan's hum. Funny how you can know something and yet not believe it's possible. Whether it's sheep cloning or space travel. Or the fact that, last night, Leo Sotolongo broke into his girlfriend's bedroom and put a bullet through her skull. Then he turned the gun on himself. Mario's words seep through my skin, but my brain is bargaining. I see only possibilities.

What if I'd answered Leo's calls? What if he'd come back to class? But it's over. Mario's stopped speaking.

"He never thought there was a problem," I say.

"You mean he wouldn't give anyone the satisfaction of admitting it, even to himself." Mario's sad voice is angry too. "It wasn't the first time he held a gun to that girl's head. The police gave it back when she dropped the charges, though. He made sure of that. He called last week, said he wanted back into class so she'd take him back. Not that he needed counseling, not him."

"What did you tell him?"

"I told him I can only help people who'll let me." Mario watches a train pull by, maybe remembering, as I am, the story Leo told us. "But that's not enough people."

I can't stay. A second later, I'm out the door, Mario's words still in my ears.

I sprint downstairs, then six blocks to the station. The escalator bears me to the platform. I can't breathe. And I'm cold. The sun bakes the red-brown tiles, suddenly so close, so bright. I shut my eyes. Neysa. What did she look like, even? But I see Caitlin's face, Caitlin's blue eyes, staring.

Could it have been me, me and Caitlin? No. I want to scream it. No! My brain tells me different.

You and Leo were the same, it says. Lonely, obsessed. Angry and out of control too. I saw it in Leo, I see it in myself. All I did to Caitlin, everything I said. Of course she's afraid of me. I'm no different from Leo. I wasn't, and I'm not.

But can I be?

Is there time?

The train's in sight, white light piercing the sun, and I think of Leo's brother. Then Leo himself, ending it when life became unbearable. It would be easy for me too. Who would care? Not Caitlin, not Tom. Not my father. One final shock, then no more pain. No pain. I feel in my pocket for the ring, Caitlin's ring. My fingers meet coldness, and I take it out, hold it to the light. Purple prisms reflect around me. The train descends. I clutch the ring. Only the ring supports me. I step toward the tracks. The horn sounds. I hoist the ring to the sky and raise my arm.

Then it's flying out, out over the track, then crashing to the street below. I watch until, finally, I can't. The train pulls in but still I see the ring. Hitting ground somewhere below, its stone shattering on impact. The doors open, and I walk inside. I collapse into a seat and stare out the window. Where is it? Where's the ring? It should be a mile wide, but it's gone. The train pulls out, and still I look. I try to picture Caitlin's face, but I can't.

I only see my own face, reflected in the glass.

3:00 A.M.—beach behind my father's house

I'm sitting here with a flashlight, Caitlin's pen, and my journal, which, in addition to being smudged, torn, and rippled, is now pretty much covered in wet sand. I have to finish it, though. I don't want to, but I have to.

The pain in my brain was at tumor level by evening. Yet, somehow, I had a front-row seat, watching Saint O'Connor and company, in wigs, dancing to "Short Shorts." Caitlin squeezed my hand, and through the deafening laughter, I heard her voice.

"I love you, Nicky. You don't have to be a football hero for me to love you."

I pushed her back, her words like a hand clutching my throat. Onstage, Saint ground his butt. I glanced away. Then, I noticed the dolphin on the calf of one of the wigged dancers. Tom. He wore a red bouffant wig, kicking and strutting with the others—

without me. They belonged together. I was the oddball. For the first time in my life, I wanted to go home. Finally, the lights came up for intermission.

"Wasn't Tom funny?" Liana said. I noticed then that the seat by hers was empty. "He wanted it to be a surprise."

I started toward the doors. Cat stood to join me, but I said, "You following me to the men's room?" She shook her head, sitting.

I stayed away a long time. When I returned, Tom and Saint were there, wigless. Caitlin was gone.

"Where's Caitlin?" I said.

"And congratulations on a fine performance to you too," Tom said. Then he saw my face. "Nick, I'd have asked you to do it with us, but you'd have said it was stupid."

"It _was_ stupid. Where's Caitlin?"

"Backstage." Liana's face was smug. "Mrs. Reyes came looking for her because she's listed to sing. We wouldn't let her wimp out."

I looked around, unable to believe she was really gone. I started to protest that she wasn't dressed to sing. Then I realized she was. The aqua dress she wore was my favorite. I thought she'd worn it for me. She wore it to sing. She'd tricked me. I rushed up the aisle and crashed through the doors.

The courtyard outside the auditorium was empty. No one saw me run across or around to the back. No one heard the pounding, screaming in my head. I beat the stage door, but no one answered. My lungs felt overfilled. I was sweating, almost crying. My knuckles throbbed. I fell to the ground, exhausted, and sat, eyes closed, seemingly for hours. Finally, I dragged myself back to the auditorium and fell into my seat.

Caitlin's solo was next. The song she sang was sexy, about love and meeting the man of her dreams. I felt every eye on her. Slut. I watched her face for some sign she meant me. Nothing. Not a glance my way. My neck muscles tightened. My eyebrows were frozen in position, my mouth paralyzed in a smile. The ungrateful bitch had betrayed me. I felt like shit, and it was her fault. All she wanted was to control me, use me. And I'd let her. I'd let her humiliate me, but this was the last time. She couldn't treat me like this.

When the lights came up, I bolted for the door.

I stood behind the auditorium, waiting. Caitlin was one of the first people out. I grabbed her arm. She turned toward me, hope written on her face.

"Did you like it, Nicky?"

I didn't answer. The door opened, and more people crowded out. Derek patted her shoulder. "Good job, Caitlin." He moved on.

"Good job." I mocked her. I yanked her away and out to my car. The parking lot was deserted. Cars were shadows, illuminated by towering light poles. I pushed her toward my car, parked near the back.

"Get in!"

She struggled against me, somehow managing to break free and run several steps before tripping. I caught her. I tried to carry her back to the car, but she yelled and kicked and thrashed against me.

We were under a light pole, our shadows

tall as dinosaurs. I threw her against it.
My mind was reeling, detached from my
body. All I could think was to show her
she couldn't do this, couldn't defy me, treat
me like I didn't matter. Caitlin's face was
white in the glow. She sunk to the ground.
All the time, her mouth moved, forming no
words. Finally, she said, "Please, Nick . . .
I . . . Mrs. Reyes said . . . and Tom and
Liana. I thought you'd like it once you
saw."

"Bitch!" I slapped her across the face
and reeled back from the force of the blow.
Her head smashed the lamppost. I stumbled,
regained my footing. I advanced on her,
yelling, "Why?"

She began to sob, holding her hand to
her cheek as if those little white fingers
would shield her. "I don't know, I don't
know." Over and over she said it.

I hit her again. This time, my fist was
clenched, my feet set. The earth shuddered
to a stop, gained momentum with my fist.
Knuckles meeting her jaw. Words streaming
forward without even knowing. Her white
hand, flying up, away from her face, no

259

protection. Fingers floating against darkness. I was small, weak. Gaining power, though. Gaining power by taking it from her and the words coursing from my throat. I hit her again, not seeing her face, couldn't make her real if I wanted. Only anger, red, violent, on me like a cloak. My hands closing around her neck, barely knowing who she was. Then she was on the ground, not even crying, whispering something I couldn't hear.

"Get up!" I screamed.

"No." I could barely hear her. "Please, Nick. No more."

"Get up!" I leaned to pull her toward me. I didn't see her face then, but I see it now, bruised, broken. Blood seeped from one nostril and out her mouth. Only her eyes were Caitlin's eyes. Caitlin's blue, blue eyes stared at me, pleading. Her hands still struggled to protect her face. I pulled her up, pulled her toward me so I could hurt her.

Someone walked by, heading for a car. And another, and another. Caitlin called weakly, and I laughed. A dozen people passed like nothing. I dragged her up again, my arm arching back. No one could stop me. Then, hands on my shoulders, pulling me away. I lost my hold, and Caitlin staggered to the ground. I turned. Knuckles met my jaw. Stumbling backward. Knees, then my head hit asphalt. Everything was black, starry. When I woke, seconds or hours later, someone was crouched over Caitlin. Others came, so many faces. Liana. Derek. But I couldn't make out the figure in the lamplight, the one holding Caitlin. The person who'd hit me.

Then I saw the dolphin silhouette on his leg.

APRIL 12

7:15 A.M.—my bedroom

"Caitlin?"

"Who's this?"

"It's me." Then, quickly at her intake of breath, "Don't worry. I'm not trying to get you to take me back."

"Will you stop calling me?" she says, over my words. "Please. I could tell—"

"Go ahead. Call the police. Have your boyfriend amputate my face. I deserve it. I deserve it. Just listen a sec, okay?"

I take her silence as agreement. Out front, someone's mowing the lawn, and I say, "Look, I know you couldn't like me anymore, not after what I did. I know that now. I just . . ." Why is this so hard? "I'm just sorry. I thought I meant it before, but I didn't know. I mean, it's like apologizing for stepping on someone's foot. You say you're sorry, but you don't really understand how bad you hurt them."

I stop talking, out of words. Caitlin fills the lull.

"So beating me up is like stepping on someone's foot?"

She sounds tired.

"No. No. I'm screwing this up and I don't deserve

you even listening to me, but I get it. I mean I understand how bad . . . how much I hurt you. How much I could have . . ." Neysa's eyes haunt me, and finally, I say, "Look, I'm just sorry. You didn't deserve what I did to you. I loved you so much, Cat."

The lawn mower stops, and silence fills the room. Caitlin's voice startles me.

"I can't believe that anymore, Nick."

The line goes dead. I hold the phone until its angry clatter reminds me to hang up.

JULY 11

Mario's class (last day!!!)

So why aren't I doing a goal-line boogie in the doorway? Who knows? Nerves, maybe. Mario said there'd be a final, and I haven't studied, haven't taken notes. I clutch my journal and thank God no one will read it.

There are five guys now. Across the circle, A.J. enlightens us about the gymnastic abilities of a girl he met at driving school, and I tune out Kelly's latest spin on why did the Cuban cross the road? I realize I know more about these guys, and they about me, than anyone I've ever met, so when Tiny sends around a phone list, I write my number—though I'll never call anyone.

It's Tiny, also, who says, "What about the final, Mario?"

Groans, but Mario silences us, saying, "Chill, *hombres*. This final's for me, not you. And there's only one question."

"What's the question?" Ray says.

Mario leans against his desk, flanked by pictures of his wife and son. "It's been six months. We've talked a lot, shared some memories, said things we wish we hadn't, maybe even made some lifelong friends. Question is: What was this class about?"

I jiggle my hand on my knee, avoiding eye contact.

Around me, there's silence, like the first day again. Finally, Ray, with his gift for stating the obvious, rescues us. "That's easy. It's about not hitting women."

Give the man a prize.

Mario says, "Okay. Who else?"

"It's not just that, right?" Tiny says. "I've been telling Donyelle all that stuff about primary emotions and expressing anger. It's that too, right?"

Mario nods. He surveys the circle, his eyes resting on each of us. An idea's forming in my head, but I don't mean to speak.

Still, it pops out. "I think it's about being a loser."

Except that wasn't what I'd meant to say.

"Who you calling a loser?" Tiny says.

I stand. "Me, Tiny. *I'm* a loser. That's what my dad says, anyway. Loser. Failure. I tried to prove him wrong, finding things I could control, like my grades. And Caitlin. When she said *no*, or I'd think there was someone else, there'd be this voice in my head, almost too soft to hear, whispering *loser. You're a loser, a mistake.* And I had to drown it out, had to win, no matter the cost." I feel a bead of sweat on my forehead. "But, what it cost was Caitlin. Hurting her made me a loser."

I sit, silence engulfing me. Beside me, Tiny and Ray eyeball their shoes. Someone speaks.

"How do you stop the voice?"

The speaker, surprisingly, is Kelly.

"My daddy says that shit, too," he adds.

"I don't know," I say. I turn to Mario. "Do you?"

Mario laces his fingers behind his head, glancing at the ceiling. Then he looks at us. "If I said it's something you have to figure out yourself, you'd call me chicken, right?" We nod, even some who won't look up, and Mario says, "Then, I guess you're ready to hear about me."

There's silence except for the sound of Mario's chair legs scraping floor tiles as he joins the circle. Then he begins.

"My wise uncle Gustavo used to say, 'You can tell a man there are fifty billion stars in the sky, and he'll believe you. But if he sees a sign saying WET PAINT, he has to check for himself.'" We all laugh at this joke we heard as kids, but Mario holds up a hand, saying, "Don't laugh at the truth. We accept without question that we—human beings—are the center of the universe. Talk about hubris. But when a woman says, 'I love you,' that won't go through our skulls."

I thought of Caitlin saying she loved me that last night. I'd barely even heard it.

"It's easy to believe what's in books or even television commercials, but no one teaches us to believe in ourselves. Our parents slept on the job there, didn't they?" He looks at me and Kelly. "They let us cry one or one hundred times too many and said we were failures until we knew it like a religion. And once you join that Church of Fear, Jesus or Buddha or Cousin Kevin's Cult of Wonders down the street may look good, but that Fear is what holds you until finally, when a woman says she loves you, you know she's lying. Or it's just a matter of time 'til she sees what you're really like and finds someone better. And that adds up to a lot of fear."

"How would you know?" I ask, glancing again at his photos.

"I know because Fear's a friend of mine," Mario says. "My father trained me in its ways from birth. Seven years ago, I was neck deep, sinking faster than burnt sugar in flan. I had my degree, my practice, and a wife who *said* she loved me. Then I started hearing my father's voice.

"Teresa wanted to have a baby. First *Papi* thought that was fine—keep her in her place. But when she started showing, he was there, whispering, 'She doesn't love you. She won't stay once the baby comes,' and I tried to drown him out, yelling louder and louder and making Teresa cry until one day, yelling wasn't enough. I pushed my pregnant wife from a moving car."

The room is silent. Mario wipes a tear, but clearly, one is all he'll allow himself. Wife and baby smile from his desk.

267

"Teresa lost the baby, and I lost Teresa. My father got off scot-free. I couldn't blame him for what I did. He wasn't there, just me. Teresa told everyone it was an accident—she learned fear at her own mama's knee, so I got away with it."

Slowly, it dawns on me. Mario was one of us, one of the walking wounded. And now—he's fine. What's to stop me from ending up like him? Nothing. "What happened?" I asked.

"Somehow," Mario says, "I ended up in a class like this, not planning on learning anything. But in the end, I retook the class. And again. And again, until finally I taught my own class. I don't have all the answers, and I don't know how to stop your voice, Nick. But hearing it is a good start."

"Hearing it?"

Mario walks to me. "Don't let that voice be your elevator music. Turn it up 'til it's like you're by the speaker at Lollapalooza. Then, turn it off and listen to something else.

"For me, the voice stopped when I decided to teach these classes, to work with men like myself. I told my father about my new life plan and got his voice in stereo. I watched him, yelling, hopping like a live fish on a frying pan, and I thought: If I met this idiot at the supermarket, I wouldn't ask his opinion about whether the tomatoes were fresh. I stopped listening that day, and after a while, the voice moved out." He looks at me. "You can't respect yourself if you're letting someone beat you up—inside or out. What you learned here is only half the equation. The other half is self-respect."

He stops talking. He sits, staring at his hands a long moment. I have something to say but, rather than interrupt him, I raise my hand. When he acknowledges it, I say, "I think I know what you've been trying to teach us." This time, I have the words I want.

He nods for me to go on, and I say, "It's about being a man, isn't it? A real man. Not just about who's bigger or stronger or who gets more women. But . . ." I stop. Everyone's looking at me, and I don't like it. I sound like a wuss.

But Mario says, "Go ahead. You're on the right track."

I think about not liking to talk with everyone's eyes on me, and I say, "It's about doing the right thing even if you don't want to do it. About taking responsibility for your actions, like you always told us." I think of Caitlin and add, "It's about letting go when you really, really want to hold on so bad."

Mario looks at me a second, then nods. "You passed the test, Nick."

I glance away. It wasn't what I wanted to learn. What

I wanted was Caitlin back, not the knowledge I'd lost her forever. But I have. How will I learn to deal with it?

Now, Mario's talking again, saying he'll report back to the court that we all completed our requirements. He dismisses us for the last time.

After everyone else leaves, I approach him.

"I want to retake the class," I say.

I expect raised eyebrows—I haven't been a model student—but he says, "Yes. I'd like that."

I tap my toes, silently, inside my shoes before saying, "See you next week, then." I start to leave, then turn back and shove my journal toward him. "Could you read this? I mean, if you have time."

He takes it. "I'll find time." Then he does something shocking. He puts the notebook on his desk and holds out his arms. I hesitate a moment before stepping toward him and letting him take me in. I've never hugged a guy before, never really held anyone but Caitlin. The warmth of it surprises me.

We finally separate. I'm out the door before I remember all the things I wrote about my father. I reach for the knob, wanting to ask for my notebook, say I was kidding about coming back.

Then I decide I don't care—I've been trying to breathe underwater too long. It's time to get some fresh air into my lungs.

JULY 11

1:00 P.M.

I'm watching television, remembering, maybe, what Mario said about self-respect or maybe my point-of-no-return gesture of giving him that notebook. That's the only way to explain the following:

My father is asleep;

A Marlins game blares on television;

My sneakers rest on the hand-carved fruitwood coffee table;

Along with a juicy can of Mountain Dew.

Thus summoned, my father enters. I don't move. He storms to the television, slaps the off button three times before it works, then kicks my feet off the table. Except he misses and hits the can instead. It flies toward the ceiling, drenching the sofa, the rug, the table, and my father in a tidal wave of piss-colored liquid. He starts yelling.

I don't move. I feel my brain short-circuiting, trying to carry me to an alternative reality. I can't go. I concentrate, instead, on Mario's words. *Respect yourself.* Mario's yelling louder than my father, and to shut him up, I look in my father's eyes. For the first time, I don't see myself.

"Clean it!" he screams between obscenities. His

face is a mask I wouldn't recognize if it didn't haunt my dreams. "Clean it, you little shit!"

"No," I say.

Outside, Biscayne Bay runs dry.

He stops midsentence then says, "What do you mean, no?"

He leans forward, his voice a roar encompassing every insult, slap, and backhand, every emotion I've felt. Memories fly, spilling evil and hope like Pandora's box, and my mind tries to avoid him, tries to run, hide even as my body won't let it. I can't go.

I can't go.

Don't go.

Don't.

I stand.

"I didn't spill it." My voice is cold.

"What?"

"I'm not cleaning it, because I didn't spill it."

The green eyes are wild with disbelief. He starts to say something, stops, then starts again. His head shakes involuntarily, his face purples. He raises his hand. I grab it. Then, the other arm. It takes all my strength to hold him, but somewhere, I find more, and I say—no—I scream:

"You are not going to hit me anymore!"

Silence.

"You are not going to hit me anymore!

"You are not going to hit me anymore, you bastard!"

I don't know how many times I scream it until, finally, I stop. His mask falls. He makes a small noise, maybe a chuckle, in the back of his throat. Our eyes meet. His are cold again. Mine burn. My face aches as if he hit me. I loosen my hold on him, and feel him pull free, arms, wrists, fingers slipping from my grasp. Not strong, not powerful, just a man. Why did I think he was so strong?

He walks away.

I sink into the Mountain Dew fallout and sit, quiet, until his shoes reach the landing. I lean back. Sun off the water streams through French doors. I hide my eyes.

I remember, now, how to cry.

SEPTEMBER 2
(MY SEVENTEENTH BIRTHDAY)

7:25 A.M.—Key Biscayne High parking lot

Junior year, my first-day déjà vu is dulled by the sense that everything's different, starting with my car. It's a silver BMW roadster, my father's latest acquisition. A week after the Mountain Dew incident, I got back from the beach with Kelly and Tiny (can you believe it?) and found my father in my room, sober, calm, almost shy. He sat on the bed, hesitating a long moment.

Finally, he said, "It is not, perhaps, the American way to be hard on one's children. I have raised you with discipline. How your *Papou* raised me."

I blurted, "How old were you when you left home?"

His eyes met mine and filled, for one instant, with crystal understanding. He walked out. I knew the answer, though. My father left home at sixteen. Never saw his family again. That day was the only time he'd mentioned my grandfather.

He didn't bring it up again, but a week later, he brought me the car keys at breakfast. For the first time in my life, he stammered. "I shouldn't have sold . . . I should . . . for your birthday." He never apologized, but the title was in my name this time. That's the best he can do.

Today, I pull beside a familiar car, Tom's white Jeep. He's alone, but I pretend not to see. Avoiding him is less gut-wrenching than being ignored. I slide my backpack off the seat and head for school.

Tom's behind me. "Nick!"

Why is he bothering me? I keep walking. He runs behind, yelling my name.

"Funny," I say, finally. "Thought I heard a voice, but no one here's speaking to me."

He catches up. "Nick . . ."

I turn to face him. His hair is short as the day I first saw him in kindergarten. He's clutching something, the spring *Seagull* literary journal. He stares at me a moment, not speaking. When I start to walk away, he says, "Caitlin thinks you wrote this." He points to a page.

"Wrote what?" But I know. It's my poem, which Higgins agreed to publish anonymously. In the fall edition, there will be two more under my name.

He points again. "This."

"So? You're breaking your vow of silence to congratulate me on my writing?"

"So, you wrote it?" When I don't answer, he adds, "Caitlin doesn't go to Key anymore. She's living with her dad. She's at some special performing arts school."

It takes me a second to hear that. Then, a minute

longer, to understand I'll probably never see her again. Finally, I say, "That's great. She loved to sing." I think I mean it. "That all?"

"You're not making this easy."

"Everything's easy for you."

"Think so, huh?" He reaches for my arm. I pull away, walking faster. We're at the chain-link fence that separates the student lot from Key Biscayne High Drive. He runs ahead and blocks the entrance. "Think it's easy finding out my best friend never told me anything about himself?"

"What are you talking about?"

"This!" He jiggles the paper in his hand. "Caitlin says you wrote this about *me*, this crap about being alone and not wanting to tell your secrets. She said you apologized, she thought you meant it this time. She told me other stuff too, about you and your dad. How could you not have told me that shit?"

"Um, I don't know. Why don't I look at you and your perfect life and just open a vein for your entertainment?"

"My life's not perfect. You know it isn't. I *told* you."

"It looked pretty perfect from where I stood."

He thinks about that and, above the anger in his eyes, I see pity I never wanted from him. I turn away. The late bell rings and, except for a few stragglers, the parking lot is silent. "Look, I have to go." I push past him and walk toward school.

He speaks to my back. "I thought we were friends."

"Some friend." I turn. "First sign of trouble, you took off."

His eyes avoid mine. "You hurt Caitlin. You hurt her bad. That's all I saw. I didn't know you were hurting too. I told you everything, and you kept this huge secret from me."

"If you'd known, you'd just have found a new best friend sooner—someone more your class."

Tom looks at me like I loogeyed in his face. "That's what you think? I'm some snob?"

"Pretty much."

He bites his lip. "Yeah, that's what Liana's family thought too. Called me the Golden Gringo, bugged her until she dumped me. But you, Nick?" He turns away, his voice a strangled whisper. "Screw you for thinking that."

He starts to cross the street, and suddenly I don't want him to leave. I yell after him, "What do you want, Tom?"

He stops, blocking traffic. "I want things like they used to be."

"They aren't."

He finishes crossing and sinks onto the curb. I

follow him. I can't say why. "I want to forgive you," he says, touching his hair. "I want you to forgive me."

I stand over him. "Why? What Caitlin told you—it doesn't change anything. It doesn't excuse it. You think I'm some mental case who's not responsible for my actions?"

"No. I don't know." He tips back his head, closing his eyes against looking at me. "Maybe it doesn't excuse it. Maybe it explains it. I don't know, maybe I wasn't a good enough friend, but I want to be."

I watch Tom, leaning back, staring at the sky now. I've always known Tom, but I never looked at him, never saw him before now. He was always Tom the athlete, Tom the most likely to . . . everything. How could I expect him to see me when I didn't see him?

"I should have told you," I say finally. "I just . . . I didn't want to lay that on you."

"You were my best friend," he says.

"I should have told you." I gesture at his hair. "You did that for Liana?"

"Doesn't matter." But he nods. "She said my dating her was a phase, like the long hair. I needed to rebel against my parents with an *oye* girlfriend." He runs a hand across his shorn head. "Sure didn't feel like a phase."

I sit beside him on the curb. "We'll start a club, Brothers in Celibacy." I hold out my hand.

He accepts it, a germ of a smile forming. "To the brotherhood."

"To the brotherhood."

We shake. I move away, saying, "She spared your feelings. She really dumped you 'cause you're ugly."

He laughs. "Hey, I just want to hang out with you to look taller by comparison."

"Asshole!"

Tom takes off running, and I follow.

Want to know what happened to Caitlin?

Read *Diva* and find out!

*L*ots of girls I know call themselves divas. "I'm such a diva!" they say, as they're rubbing your nose in some five-hundred-dollar shoes their daddy bought them. But being a diva's a lot more than just being a rich grrrl. It's about singing, about getting flowers thrown onstage—about being brilliant. I plan to be a diva someday. But first, I have to get through this audition.

And—wouldn't you know it—there's a wad of phlegm stuck in my throat.

The scene: I'm in an auditorium with, maybe, fifty other wannabes, trying out for the musical theater program at Miami High School of the Arts. Goths sit with goths, punk rockers with punk rockers. The girl next to me has an eyebrow-ring and hair Jell-O–dyed acid red. Everyone here has something freaky about them . . . except me. I'm the one and only person here in a dress (which maybe *is* freaky).

And I bet I'm the only one here with gunk in my throat.

Don't think about it. But I can feel it lying behind my tongue like cafeteria spaghetti, at a life-changing audition. I clear my throat and Eyebrow-Ring Girl gives me a look and nods at the person onstage.

'Scuse me—I'll choke more quietly in the future.

I sneak another look at her. My cheerleader friends would say she probably isn't getting enough attention at home. But I think anyone who'd wear that outfit has to be cool, and I wonder what it would be like to *want* to be noticed.

Me, I'm all about not being noticed. I'm sixteen, and for the first fifteen, I was a fatgirl, invisible as they come. I was okay with that. Well, maybe not okay, but . . . used to it. But last summer, I went to fat camp and lost thirty-five pounds, and became (at least temporarily) a *thin* girl, a blond prettygirl. I actually made the homecoming court and dumped the hottest guy in school . . . and still became one with the walls most days.

If any of my friends knew I was here, auditioning for a performing arts school, *that* they'd notice. In a *bad* way. But I didn't tell them. I didn't even tell my mother. This is the first time in my life I've ever done anything all by myself.

There's a bunch of reasons for that.

First, my friends all want me to be like them—cheerleaders, homecoming queens. I thought by losing weight I *could* be like that. But now, even though I'm thin enough, I'm still not cheerleader material. Funny, changing how I looked didn't change who I *am*. I picture myself doing a pyramid or making up a cheer and . . . *oh, puke.*

"See anything interesting?"

Too late, I realize I'm still staring at the girl with the eyebrow ring. *I am a dorkus maximus.*

"Um . . . I love your hair."

"What are you doing?" she asks.

I stare at her. Is it *that* obvious I don't belong here? Is it the dress?

"For the audition? *Habla ingles?* What are you performing?"

"Oh . . . I sing . . . opera." I wait for her to laugh or make a snarky comment.

"Cool." She raises her pierced eyebrow. "You have one of those horn helmets?"

I make the face Mom calls my diva face—eyeballs up; trying not to snort. "Um, not yet."

"Sorry. It's just, you don't look like an opera singer. You're not . . ."

"Fat?" *No. Not anymore.*

The girl laughs. "That's not what I was going to say."

But I know it was. It always is.

The woman up front calls a name (not mine). Eyebrow-Ring Girl turns to look.

Opera is the second reason I'm here. I love it. Most people think opera is a weird thing. Probably so. But it's *my* weird thing—the one thing I'm really good at. Maybe good enough to get a dessert named after me someday (Peaches Melba was named after a diva) or maybe a town. Maybe even good enough to get into this school.

The biggest, hugest reason I'm here (*and* the reason I'd never tell anyone) is my ex-boyfriend. I need to go somewhere where everyone hasn't already heard the sad, sad saga of me and Nick. And also, where I don't have to see him every day.

I pop a cough drop into my mouth and make myself sit still for two whole minutes, until the girl who's auditioning finishes singing.

Omigod! What if I'm next?

"Sean Griffin," the woman up front calls.

I actually really, really wanted to be next.

I read a book about auditioning. It said the worst thing that could happen in an audition is that you don't get the part, so you have no money, so you can't buy food, so you die. Like . . . if you thought that the absolute worst thing that could happen at an audition was *death*, then you'd be less nervous about screwing up.

That so did *not* make me feel better.

"Here I am!" a voice sings.

The guy, Sean Griffin, is skinny and wears a purple unitard, which seriously clashes with his blond hair, and eyes so blue I can see them even from a distance. He looks older, and he's been standing with the teachers, so I thought he was an assistant or something. Guess he's just a suck-up. He walks onstage, plunks a Burger King crown on his head (Really!), and starts to sing.

Everything has its season. Everything has its time.
Show me the reason and I'll soon show you a rhyme!

As soon as he starts singing, I'm nervous. I mean, *more* nervous. Lots of people at the audition were good. But Sean Griffin is the first person who's like a professional, even in that geeky outfit. I now know why he was standing up there with the teachers, like he belonged there. He knows he's going to get in.

I wish I was confident like that. I know I'm good, but sometimes, when everyone's staring, I wonder if it's just some dumb idea, thinking I'm good *enough.*

He finishes singing, and the applause is wild. He smiles like he's used to it.

"Caitlin McCourt!"

Now, it's my turn. My throat feels worse. I wonder if it could be all in my head. Is there such a thing as psychosomatic mucus?

"Caitlin McCourt?"

"Here." I start toward the front of the auditorium.

Onstage, the accompanist says, "Hey, how about a bathroom break?"

"Oh." The teacher looks at her watch. "Okay. Caitlin, do you need an accompanist, or do you have a tape?"

I glance at the sheet music in my hands for *Phantom of the Opera*. But I've done the hardest part, I want to tell them, the standing up and walking down and having everyone stare at me in my too-cute dress part. I turn back around.

"I can play for her." The guy, Sean, is reaching for my sheet music.

"Oh, that's okay. I can wait. I wouldn't want . . ."

"No worries. I can play anything. I'm a great sight reader." He takes my book and flips it open to the page where I've had my thumb jammed for the past hour. "This?"

When I nod, he glances at the book. "Hard stuff."

"I can wait if you can't play it." Except if I sit now, I might never get back up.

"I meant hard for you. This goes up to a C above high C, doesn't it? That's way high. Are you that good?"

Wow, thanks. That really helps me feel less nervous.

Actually, I've had that C for over a year. I write down the dates when I add new notes to my range. High C was last March 13. Now I'm working on E-flat.

"Come on, Caitlin. It's Caitlin, right?" Sean puts his hand on my shoulder and guides me toward the stage. My legs are all shaking.

My legs always used to shake when I sang. It hasn't happened in a while . . .

Flashback: Me. Sixth grade. Looking like I might explode out of my jeans any second at middle-school orientation. I was with Mom (big mistake). I was signing up for chorus. The music teacher, Mrs. Hauser, said I could either go for Girls' Chorus—no audition required—or try for Concert Choir, which was mostly eighth-graders.

"Girls' chorus sounds fun. Right, Caitlin?" Mom stopped fiddling with the purple alligator clip in her hair and started toward the sign-up sheet on the piano. She was wearing hot pink size-one capris and a tube top. Doesn't everyone's mother?

"Wait. I don't want to be in Girls' Chorus. I mean, I do want to be, if that's all I can be in, but I want to be in Concert Choir. I mean, I want to try."

Mom had moved away from the sign-up sheet and was nudging me, all, "Caitlin, sweetie, there's an *audition*. That means you'd have to sing in front of everybody. By yourself."

"I know. I heard her. I get it."

"But honey pie, you can't sing by yourself in front of everyone. You're . . ."

Fat. I heard it even though she didn't say it. I heard her thinking it.

"You're shy . . . you've never sung in front of anyone in your life, dear."

"Can I try?" I asked Mrs. Hauser, not Mom.

"Of course you can."

"Are you sure, honey?" Mom said. "I have appointments. You heard what she said. It's all eighth-graders."

Mrs. Hauser stood there with an oh-god-don't-make-me-get-involved-in-this look. I faced Mom down for the first time ever.

"I'm staying." I took the pen from Mrs. Hauser and wrote my name on the audition sheet. I joined the kids in the corner, and Mom sat down.

When Mrs. H. called my name, I wanted to run. Mom was right. It was one thing to sing in my room. It was a completely 'nother thing to sing in front of fifty people—and not one of them looked like a sixth-grader. But I walked up, feeling like Snow White in the movie—pre-dwarves—when she's dumped in the forest and all those eyes are looking at her from the darkness. My legs were shaking so hard I thought I'd fall over.

I closed my eyes, opened my mouth, and started to sing.

The world didn't end. Halfway through, my legs stopped shaking.

I opened my eyes.

In *Snow White*, when the A.M. hours come, Snow realizes that the scary eyes in the night are really gentle woodland creatures. That's how I felt that day. The people in that room were looking at me, but not in a bad way. I'd never met them, but they were like friends. They wanted to know me because I was good. I was really good. At that moment, maybe I was even a little visible.

I made Concert Choir that day—the *only* sixth-grade girl who did, thank you very much—and since then I've made most things I've tried out for.

Here and now: My legs are shaking so hard I can barely stand, so I lean against the piano like those opera singers on PBS. I'm calm. Really. I breathe. You're good at breathing, Caitlin. Very good. You *practice* breathing for opera.

"Are you ready . . . Caitlin?" Sean says my name real soft.

I nod. If I could still close my eyes, I would. But of course, I'd look like a complete dork if I did that.

Right before the music starts is the quietest time in the world. I can hear other people breathing. Then my song. I can feel it in my body. It's too late to back out now. It's sing or be forever known as the girl who ran away in the middle of the audition.

Concentrate!

In the song, Christine's this opera singer who's possessed by the Phantom of the Opera. He sings through her, from inside her, making his voice come through hers. I try to feel the Phantom singing through me, locked inside me, making my voice climb higher, higher, until my muscles hurt from breathing. *Up!* I think, as I was taught, forcing the voice into my head, and through it all, I feel the Phantom inside me, hear his voice, screaming, "Sing, my Angel of Music! Sing to me!" like the voice on the CD. It seems so real, and my voice climbs higher, higher, and only when it gets to the highest note do I realize that the Phantom's voice *is* real; it's not just in my head. It's Sean Griffin's voice behind me at the piano.

I gasp out my last note, a high C, and it's over.

Then silence again.

Then applause. *Big* applause.

Sean grins at me from the piano bench. I grin back.

Okay. So I can, on occasion, rock.

Back in my seat, I listen to the fifth girl to sing "On My Own" from *Les Miz*. She's also the worst. I feel bad for her. Then the girl with the eyebrow ring, who does the witch's rap from *Into the Woods*, and who is so good I sort of hate her, and a six-foot-tall football player type who actually sings "I Whistle a Happy Tune" from *The King and I* badly while everyone tries not to lose it.

And then it's over. "You'll hear one way or the other next month," the director tells us. "Thanks for coming."

People start leaving. I want to say something to Eyebrow-Ring Girl, compliment her on how incredible she was, but she's already gone. I stoop to pick up my music.

"Hey," a voice says behind me.

I look up. It's Sean Griffin. People are walking out.

"Hi," I say. "Um, thanks for playing for me."

"No problem. You need a ride somewhere?"

I took the train here, and I have to take a bus home from the train station. But I can't get in a car with some guy I don't know, just because he's a good singer. With my luck with guys, he'll turn out to be a perv or a serial killer.

"Uh, no thanks," I say. "My mom's picking me up."

"Oh, okay." He grins. Up close, his eyes aren't really blue, but they're not green either. I wonder if they've changed since I first looked. Weird.

"Bye." He walks away. When he reaches the door, he says, "Hey, Caitlin."

"What?"

"I'll see you at school."

It takes me a second to realize he means *this* school. I laugh. "Oh . . . if I get in."

He laughs too. But he says, "You will. With a voice like that, you can do anything you want."

He's gone before I can say anything else. I look around. The room's cleared out, and I'm all alone. The sun's streaming through the dirty windows, and I watch Sean as he goes to the street. Then I watch his back until he is totally swallowed up by the glare.

♪ Opera_Grrrl's Online Journal

Subject: Hi!
Date: April 5
Time: 9:37 p.m.
Feeling: Thoughtful

Weight: 115 lbs. this morning (Eek!)
Days Since I Auditioned for Miami HS of the Arts: 23

Okay, so here's the deal. My former shrink, Lucia (*long* story), was after me 2 keep a journal. "Write your thoughts," she said. "U don't have 2 show anyone."

i.e, a pointless exercise. No thx! I do enough of those in SCHOOL!

Besides, who wants a notebook where anyone can read my "thoughts?" Like, what if I got hit by a bus??? I can just picture it: Mom, drumming her pink-manicured nails on my hosp. bed, all "Oh, sugar dumpling, I know u feel bad, but could u possibly explain this little thing on page 15?" Again: No thx!

But some of my friends started keeping these online journal things, & I thought that would be better. The anonymous thing is cool. The *world* can read it, but my ex-boyfriend, Internet stalkers, etc. ("etc." meaning my mother), won't know it's me. The journal name, Opera_Grrrl, is my secret identity. Think Clark Kent/Superman, Bruce Wayne/Batman.

Okay . . . . some important details:
Name: Well, I'm not going 2 tell you that (see above)
Age: 16

Occupation: Student @ a high school in Fla. (but thinking about making a change)

Hobbies/Interests: See above . . . . I love 2 sing!!!

Pet Peeves: People who think my hobbies & interests are weird

Dating Status: Unattached

The question ur all wondering about (even tho probably no 1 is reading this): The reason I had a therapist is b/c I recently broke up w/ the boyfriend from HELL!!!

What is the Boyfriend from Hell? It is one who seems really perfect:

· wicked-hot
· nice car
· showed up on time
· brought flowers
· wrote poetry

But also:

· hit me
· told me I was fat
· said I should only hang out w/ his friends b/c mine were all losers
· said no one would ever want 2 be w/ me but him
· said my singing was stupid
· and, um, did I mention, HIT ME???

So this past Dec., I broke up w/him, & I actually went 2 court and got a piece of paper that says if he comes 2 close, I can call the cops & they will throw his butt in jail.

That's when I got the shrink. I went for a month or 2, sat in a circle w/other girls who'd had bad boyfriends, talked about them, wrote poetry about them, did interpretive dances about them, role-played what we'd say if we saw them, cried, etc., etc., etc . . . . then I got tired of wallowing in my problems so I stopped going. I use the time for practicing my singing now. *That's* therapy.

But every once in a while, I think about getting back together w/Nick. How wacko does that make me???

Which is why I'm also thinking about switching schools.